THE EMBANKMENT MURDER

A man's body is found on the Embankment missing a canine tooth, which
turns up nearby on the ground. It is the
first in a chain of grotesque murders
that all involve the same M.O.; though
on subsequent occasions, the tooth has
been taken. Out of his depth, Detective Inspector Evens of Scotland Yard
calls in London's foremost amateur
criminologist, Professor Barrington.
What is the connection between the
murdered men — and can Barrington
bring the criminal to justice before he
himself is added to the tally of the
dead?

GERALD VERNER

THE EMBANKMENT MURDER

Complete and Unabridged

LINFORD
Leicester

First published in Great Britain

First Linford Edition
published 2019

Copyright © 1934 by Gerald Verner
Copyright © 2018 by Chris Verner

A catalogue record for this book is available
from the British Library.

ISBN 978–1–4448–4270–8

Published by
F. A. Thorpe (Publishing)
Anstey, Leicestershire

Set by Words & Graphics Ltd.
Anstey, Leicestershire
Printed and bound in Great Britain by
T. J. International Ltd., Padstow, Cornwall

This book is printed on acid-free paper

1

In the Fog

With the coming of sunset, a thick fog had descended upon London, blotting out landmarks like a sponge drawn across a slate, and turning the great metropolis into a seemingly dead city about which nature already appeared to have wrapped a shroud preparatory to consigning it to its last resting place.

Here and there, where the fitful gleam of a street lamp cast a dim flash of radiance, a shapeless figure seemed to detach itself occasionally from the enveloping mist, loom grotesquely for a moment in the light, and, phantom-like, vanish the next instant, becoming once more a part of the surrounding vapour from which it had emerged.

Even the ordinary sounds of the West End seemed to have become curiously hushed and muffled, as though mourning the departed spirit of the dead, and the prosaic hooting of the motor horns and sirens from the river, blended together and merged themselves into an accompanying dirge.

Somewhere high up, lost in the fog, Big Ben boomed out the hour of midnight, and the sonorous notes of the great bell were muffled and husky, as if it, too, like the rest of humanity, unable to withstand the rawness of the night, had covered up its mouth to prevent the penetrating fog from getting down its throat.

Feeling its way cautiously, like a monstrous blind beetle, a taxi turned into Bridge Street from the direction of Victoria and started, at a crawling pace, to cross Westminster Bridge. Opposite the steps which lead down to the Albert Embankment, it swung into the kerb and drew to a standstill. The door opened and a tall man in light overcoat, a white muffler concealing the lower part of his face, stepped out. Slipping some coins into the ready palm of the driver, and pulling the brim of his soft felt hat further down over his eyes, he shouted a cheery good night and crossed the road towards the steps leading down to the Embankment.

The taxi driver, cheerfully whistling a popular foxtrot decidedly out of tune, glanced at the money in his hand in the light of the lamp which shone on the meter. This seemed to put him in still brighter humour than heretofore, for his whistle increased in shrillness and tune-lessness, and after lighting the stump of a cigarette, which he removed from behind one ear, he slipped in the clutch and drove slowly off in the direction of Westminster Bridge Road. As he did so, a dark figure emerged from the shadow of the cab and slunk across the road towards St. Thomas's Hospital, where it was swallowed up in the fog.

The man in the light coat reached the bottom of the steps and paused to light a cigar. The light from the match, shining on his face, revealed a handsome man of middle age with a square-cut determined chin, a well-shaped nose, aquiline, with finely chiselled nostrils, and a mouth, the thin firm-set lips of which a carefully trimmed moustache, plentifully flecked with grey, failed to conceal.

The noisy blast of a siren from the river close at hand made him start and drop the match as he finished lighting his cigar, and he started to grope his way along the Embankment. The fog swirled and eddied around him in thin wispy streaks like phantom fingers, and he shivered slightly and pulled the muffler closer round his neck as the penetrating dampness found its way beneath his thin coat.

Stealthily, silently, like a veritable spirit of the fog itself, the other figure that had followed him across the road crept down the steps in his wake. There was something sinister, vaguely menacing, about this black shadowy form as it slunk noiselessly behind the man in the light coat, hugging the wall and taking advantage of every shadow to conceal its movements.

Some sixth sense seemed to warn the man in front of the presence of this unseen follower, for every now and again he turned his head and looked back over his shoulder. Was it intuition, premonition, or reality? It seemed as if he felt that someone was dogging his footsteps; an uncanny feeling of a presence around him! Once he stopped and strained his ears to listen, but all was silent save for the distant rumble of a belated bus, its horn sounding incessantly, and the soft lapping of the river against the Embankment, accompanied by the occasional creaking of the old barges moored alongside as they rose and fell on the swell of the tide.

Apparently satisfied that he had been mistaken, he continued on his way, humming broken snatches of a tune below his breath. Big Ben chimed the quarter as he drew near to where Lambeth Bridge crosses the Embankment. He only became aware of its nearness by the deeper shadow which it threw across the darkness of the pavement. As he stepped into this shadow, he stopped again and looked back. Again came the feeling that he was being watched. Was there someone along the Embankment behind him, or was it merely a trick of the fog? His eyes narrowed and his brows gathered in sharp furrows as he strove to pierce the impenetrable vapour. Yes — somewhere ahead of him a vague indefinable shape had moved! It was barely distinguishable close against the wall and creeping noiselessly towards him!

He advanced towards it, but had scarcely taken two strides when the figure broke into a run. The next instant the shadowy form was on him! There was a crash as the two figures met. One muffled cry tried to spring into birth and force its way from between his lips, but was checked by the strangling fingers which found their way to his throat! The two figures swayed backwards and forwards, struggling violently, and finally fell to the ground.

The right arm of the figure in black rose and fell, and the man in the light coat gave one convulsive struggle and lay still. The man in black rose to his feet, panting, and stood still for a second listening intently, then swiftly bent over the man on the ground. The light of an electric torch flashed, glinted for a moment, and went out, flashed again, and this time shone on some bright object which the man in black held in his right hand. Bending over the body, he worked quickly, every movement sure and accurate, with not a wasted second. Barely a minute had passed since he had sprung upon the man in the light coat and knocked him down. At last, with a grunt of satisfaction, he examined a small object which he held in the light of his torch in what appeared to be a pair of pliers.

After a second or two, he flung it from him with a muttered curse and switched out his torch. His hands started to move quickly, swift as lightning, over the body of his victim. Suddenly he sprang to his feet to listen, every faculty tense, alert, and strained, his body thrown a little forward. What was that? Along the Embankment, the way he had come, came the sound of measured footsteps!

Swiftly the figure in black moved further into the darkness under the bridge. Nearer came the steps — still nearer. A faint shadow scarcely distinguishable from the other shadows seemed to melt away into the fog and was lost.

From somewhere down the river came the long wail of a siren, answered nearer at hand by the hoot of a tug.

Big Ben chimed the half-hour!

2

Detective Inspector Evens Seeks Advice

Professor Barrington rose from his writing desk and, crossing to the book-case, replaced the books of reference which he had been using.

'Now, my dear Evens,' he murmured, sinking into a large armchair and twisting the massive signet ring on his first finger, 'what brings you here so early, eh?'

Detective Inspector Evens of Scotland Yard finished gulping the hot coffee which had been handed him by Barrington's secretary, and putting the cup back on the table, ran his stubby fingers through the bristling hair which stood up like a scrubbing brush from his bullet head. It was a cold raw morning, and Evens had arrived just as Barrington and his secretary were finishing an article due at the publisher's at noon, and had been glad of the steaming hot coffee which

Barrington had rang for and insisted upon his drinking.

'It's murder, Professor,' he answered in reply to the scientist's question, 'and the strangest case I've ever come up against; that's why I came to you. I know you're interested in anything that presents features out of the ordinary, and this case is bristling with 'em. It absolutely beats me.'

The professor nodded his leonine head and indicated that he was to go on. 'I shall be only too pleased if I can be of any assistance, Evens,' he said. 'Let me have all the details.'

Inspector Evens fished in an inner pocket and produced a bulky notebook. 'It happened early this morning,' he said, 'so there's no account in the papers, but I expect the evening editions'll be full of it. I've got most of the facts here.'

He consulted his notebook, and Professor Barrington settled himself comfortably in his chair, his fingers still twisting his ring.

'Shortly after half past twelve this morning,' Evens went on, 'Constable

Partridge, whose beat extends along the Albert Embankment, stumbled over something just under Lambeth Bridge. As you know, the fog was very thick, one of the densest we've had, and at first he wondered what it was that had tripped him up. Flashing on his lantern, he discovered that it was a man. Concluding that it was a drunken roisterer who'd lost his way in the fog, Partridge bent down and shook him, and found that he'd been stabbed! Partridge immediately summoned assistance and the body was conveyed to the mortuary. The man was well dressed in evening clothes, and nothing had been removed from his pockets, although in his note-case was a considerable sum of money. Therefore it doesn't look as though robbery was the motive for the crime, unless the murderer was disturbed before he had a chance of removing anything.'

Professor Barrington looked up quickly. 'Did Partridge hear anything just before he found the body?'

'I asked him that. He heard nothing.'

'And from which direction did he come along the Embankment?'

'From the Westminster end.'

'And nobody passed him on his way?'

'No, he neither heard nor saw anyone.'

The professor nodded thoughtfully, and Inspector Evens continued. 'All the man's belongings, as far as I could see,' he said, 'were intact, and his card-case contained several cards bearing the name James Lessard — Junior Constitutional Club.'

'Lessard — Lessard,' repeated Barrington. 'Not Lessard the explorer?'

'No,' answered Evens, shaking his head. 'This man's much older. I've seen photographs of Lessard, and there's no likeness between the two. Of course, he may be some sort of relation. We're making enquiries about that now. But I haven't told you yet the most extraordinary feature of the whole affair. On examining the body, it was discovered that the murderer had torn out the left canine tooth!'

A quick gleam of interest sprang into Barrington's dark eyes, and he sat slightly forward in his chair. 'How do you know it was pulled out by the murderer?' he asked.

'Because it was found a yard or two away from the body. Look!'

He took from his pocket a small object wrapped in tissue paper. Removing the covering, he held it out to Barrington. The scientist took it and carefully examined it. It was a tooth, white and entirely free from decay, the roots still moist, and slightly bloodstained.

'Unless this was removed by an expert dentist,' said Barrington, 'it must have required a considerable amount of strength and taken a fair time. Were the gums of the dead man much torn?'

'No,' answered Evens. 'The murderer seems to have made a fairly clean job of it.'

'The inference being that it was a job which he was used to.'

Barrington took a powerful lens from a drawer in the desk, and, walking over to the window, closely scrutinised the tooth through it.

'I myself have some slight knowledge of dentistry,' he remarked after several seconds had passed in silence, 'and I'm convinced that this tooth was not removed by an amateur. It was done in one swift operation, and the canine teeth are the most difficult of all to extract.'

'But in the name of sense,' snorted Evens, 'why did he want to pull out the man's tooth? It's the most absurd thing I've ever heard of! To murder a man in order to pull his teeth out! Why?'

'If you knew that, you would in all probability be able to lay your hands on the criminal,' replied Barrington, putting his lens back in his pocket and returning the tooth to Evens.

'It looks to me like the work of a madman,' said Evens. 'I can't think of any sensible explanation to account for it.'

'It's too early yet to start forming theories,' said Barrington, 'but I could supply you with half a dozen that would cover the facts. Hertford,' he added, turning to his secretary, 'will you please phone down to the garage and ask them to send the car round at once.'

'Certainly, sir.'

'I should like to have a look at the body,' continued Barrington, turning to Evens, 'and also the scene of the crime, although I expect by now any traces that may have existed will have been obliterated by the footsteps of passers-by.'

'We can stop at Lambeth Bridge on the way to the mortuary.'

Professor Barrington was unable to resist the solving of a crime no matter what other work he had on hand. It was a hobby with him, a fact which Scotland Yard had more than once been glad to take advantage of.

'I suppose you have found out where Lessard lived?' he enquired, 'and something of his habits?'

Evens nodded. 'He had a small bachelor flat in Half Moon Street.'

'Humph!' said Barrington thoughtfully, reaching out his hand and taking a cigar. 'Doesn't it strike you as peculiar that he should have been on the Albert Embankment, which is a considerable distance from Piccadilly, at all at that hour of the morning?'

'Oh, I don't know,' answered Evens, helping himself to a cigar from the box which Barrington had pushed across to him. 'He was probably returning from some visit or other.'

'Possibly. But he would hardly have chosen to walk home, particularly on such an unpleasant night. No, I think the first point to be discovered is what he was doing on the Albert Embankment, and we may find some clue to that at his flat. I think we'll go on there after we've seen the body.' Hertford, who, after phoning had gone to the window, suddenly turned round.

'The car's at the door, sir,' he announced.

Eustace Barrington crossed to the door. 'I won't keep you a minute, Evens,' he said as he went out of the room. 'Get your coat on, Hertford. I think this case will interest you.'

In less than a minute Barrington returned, and pausing to slip a few things into his pocket from a drawer in his desk, led the way down the stairs and out of the front door. The man who had brought the car round from the garage got out and touched his hat as Hertford took his place at the wheel, with Barrington beside him, Inspector Evens occupying the tonneau.

Hertford touched the self-starter and the perfectly tuned engine purred into life, and in a few seconds they were spinning down Welbeck Street into the direction of Westminster. It was a perfect winter morning, cold, but with a healthy tang in the air. The sun had emerged from the early-morning mist and was flooding the streets with light, and such a power had its rays upon human nature that as they rested upon the occupants of the car, they almost forgot the dark sinister business upon which they were engaged and gave themselves up to the enjoyment of the beauty of the morning.

Bobbie Hertford was an expert driver, and under his guiding hand the long grey car hummed along, twisting in and out of the traffic with an almost uncanny sense until, in an incredibly short space of time, they arrived at the Lambeth Bridge end of the Albert Embankment. Swinging the car into the kerb, Hertford brought it to a halt and sprang out, followed by Barrington and Evens. As they approached the bridge, a constable who was standing there saluted Evens.

'Well, Morgan,' said the inspector, 'anything fresh?'

The constable shook his head. 'No, sir. I haven't seen anyone from the Yard since you left this morning.'

Evens grunted in reply, and turning to Barrington and Hertford, pointed to a spot on the pavement directly under the bridge where an ominous stain was still visible. 'That's the spot, Professor Barrington,' he said.

Barrington's dark eyes, so long used to examining minute bacilli, swept the place in a swift, comprehensive glance. The habitual slightly bored expression which he usually possessed had given place to one of intense virility. His well-chiselled nostrils quivered like a hound on the scent, and his whole personality radiated an atmosphere of intense alertness. Those people who only knew him as man with a quietly acute scientific brain would have witnessed a revelation if they could have seen him as a hunter of men.

With his head bent forward, he searchingly examined the pavement round the bloodstains, and suddenly a little gleam crept into his eyes. Dropping on to one knee, he poked gently with his forefinger at a crack in the paving, and, after probing for a second, picked something up. Hertford, who had been watching eagerly, sprang forward.

'What have you found, sir?' he asked excitedly.

Barrington rose and dusted the knee of his trousers. 'Nothing much, my boy,' he answered, and extending his hand, showed a tiny circle of metal that glinted in the palm. Inspector Evens peered at it and grunted.

'What's that, Professor?' he asked.

The scientist smiled. 'It's a platinum link. Part, I should say, of the connecting chain of a cuff-link, or possibly a watch chain, but I'm more inclined to think a cuff-link. Of course, it may have nothing whatever to do with the ease, but there are distinct traces of a struggle having taken place, and it's quite possible that the link was snapped during that struggle. What links had Lessard?'

'Plain gold ones, as far as I can remember,' replied Evens, 'but that link may have been there for days.'

Barrington shook his head. 'No,' he objected. 'The blood has run into the crack from which I took this link, and if the link had been there before, it would have been covered by the blood, whereas it's only stained on its lower half, which shows that it fell into the crack after the blood had run in.'

'By Jove! You're right,' commented Evens. 'Then it must have been dropped by the assassin.'

'Unless,' put in Hertford, 'it dropped from someone who passed early this morning, after the body had been removed.'

'In that case,' said Barrington, turning to Hertford, 'it would not have been stained; the blood would have been dry, since the body was discovered shortly after twelve thirty, and Partridge states that no one passed along the Embankment after that until early this morning.'

Hertford nodded in agreement as Barrington slipped the little piece of metal into his silver match box.

'By the way, Evens,' continued the scientist, 'where did you discover the tooth?'

'Here, Professor.' The Scotland Yard man pointed to a place close up against the wall, and where a faint smear of blood was still visible.

Barrington twisted his ring rapidly round his finger, and his eyes travelled along the Embankment in the direction of Westminster, until they rested upon where a group of two or three workmen were engaged in relaying part of the pavement. For some minutes, he gazed abstractedly at them while Evens shuffled impatiently with his feet. To Hertford, who knew the professor's every mood, it was a sign that the keen analytical brain was at work, that facile brain which, like a highly sensitive machine, sifted fact after fact and formed theory upon theory until it had constructed one that fitted all the facts, and which therefore eventually proved to be the correct solution of the problem.

Suddenly Barrington turned round. 'Were those men at work there yesterday, or did they only start this morning?' he asked.

'When did they start, Morgan?' enquired Evens. 'You were on duty here yesterday, weren't you?'

'Yes, sir,' answered the constable. 'They've been there, only a little higher up, for the past two days.'

Eustace Barrington thanked him with a nod, and turned to Evens. 'I don't think there's anything more to be learnt here. Let's go on to the mortuary.'

They arrived at the dismal building in less than ten minutes, and already a small army of reporters, notebooks in hand, had arrived. A circle of them gathered round Inspector Evens as soon as he entered.

'Don't crowd around me now,' he snorted gruffly as he shouldered his way through, Barrington and Hertford following close on his heels. 'See you all presently.'

The divisional surgeon, Doctor Cattell, whom Barrington had met before, came forward to meet them, and conducted them into the inner room and across to where an inanimate form lay on a stone slab, covered with a white sheet.

The professor stepped quickly across, and bending down, gently turned back the sheet.

'Death must have been instantaneous,' said Doctor Cattell. 'The knife passed through his heart, severing the left ventricle.'

'I should like to see the weapon,' said the scientist, 'and also the contents of the pockets.'

Evens led the way over to a table on which was spread out a small array of articles consisting of a wallet of crocodile skin bound with gold, a gold watch and chain, a gold card case, one or two letters, a small heap of silver and coppers, a pair of gold cuff-links, and a long thin knife. Barrington picked up the cuff-links first and closely examined them. They were intact.

'The link could not have come from these, Evens,' he murmured, gently turning over the other articles. At last he turned his attention to the knife, and after looking at it for a moment, he turned to Doctor Cattell. 'This is something in your line,' he said. 'Unless I'm much mistaken, this is a surgeon's knife.'

'You're quite right, Professor,' agreed the doctor. 'It's a knife used for trephining.'

Barrington's eyes narrowed and his fore-head wrinkled up as he thoughtfully gazed at the weapon. Then he picked up the wallet and glanced through its contents. There was a considerable sum of money in notes, but nothing else. Neither the card case nor the letters yielded any result. One was a tailor's bill, and the other was merely an invitation to dine with a man who signed himself A. De Castro.

An attendant entered at this moment, to inform Inspector Evens that Scotland Yard wanted him on the 'phone.

Grumbling, the worthy inspector departed in the wake of the attendant, and Barrington walked over again to the slab on which the body lay. The scientist took from his pocket a powerful lens, and bending down, closely examined the mouth, gently turning back the upper lip so that the cavity from which the tooth had been extracted was exposed to view.

From there he next proceeded to make a careful inspection of the dead man's shoes, particularly the soles. They were a light pair of dress shoes, of patent leather. After a second or two, Barrington straightened up, and there was a faint gleam of satisfaction in his eyes.

'I think, Hertford — ' he began when Inspector Evens re-entered the room: his face was crimson, and his breath came in sharp pants as he strove to keep down his excitement.

'Professor — ' He jerked out the words like bullets from a machine gun, ' — this case beats everything! Just been on the phone to the Yard — they've had a message. James Lessard, the explorer — from his house at Reigate — ' His breath gave out, and it took a few seconds before he could recover himself.

'Well?' said Eustace Barrington, a curious light of interest in his dark eyes.

'He was found stabbed early this morning in his study,' continued Evens, 'and his left canine tooth had been extracted!'

3

The Missing Tooth

Copthorn House stood among a riot of
vegetation in heavily wooded grounds. A
low rambling house, badly in need of repair,
it looked as if it had lost its way among
the masses of clinging ivy and creeper
which covered it, and lacking the energy
to try and extricate itself from their embrace,
had settled down to slumber lazily, retreat-
ing further and further into its nest of
leaves as year succeeded year.

Where once had been well-kept lawns
and trim gravelled paths, was now a mass
of riotous weeds and decaying vegetation
which straggled over the paths and mingled
with the moss and weeds which grew everywhere in dense patches, so that scarcely a
trace of the original gravel remained visible. The whole place breathed an air of
neglect and decay, indescribably depress-
ing, in which even the warm red rays of a

setting winter sun failed to wake any semblance of animation or cheerfulness.

As Eustace Barrington's big car turned into the scarcely discernible drive through the broken and rotting gates, one of which lay half off its hinges, Bobbie Hertford surveyed the house with a look of disgust.

'Nice cheerful sort of place this is, sir,' he said. 'Sort of place which makes one feel full of the joy of spring — I think not.'

'Which in any case would be far from easy, my dear Hertford, considering that it's the middle of November,' remarked the professor with a dry smile as he tried vainly to discover where the drive ended and the bordering flower-beds began. They were running now under a closely interwoven tunnel of branches, and across the path strayed thick tendrils of what at one time had evidently been arches of rambler roses.

'Fancy anyone in their sober senses living here!' exclaimed Inspector Evens as a straying bramble jerked away his hat, and he just saved it from falling out of the car on to the path. 'I don't see anything to laugh at.' He frowned, as Hertford broke into a chuckle.

'Excuse me, Evens, but you would if there was a mirror handy,' Hertford retorted with a laugh.

'This is hardly the time to be funny, Mr. Hertford,' Evens remarked.

'Oh, I bubble over like that on any old occasion,' Hertford replied, and the Scotland Yard man grunted as he pressed his hard bowler hat further down on to his bullet head.

By this time, they had emerged from the avenue of overhanging trees. Facing them was a flight of dilapidated stone steps at the top of which was a heavy door, the paint blistered and peeling with the heat of many summers' exposure to the sun. This evidently was the main entrance to the house.

Barrington pulled the car up opposite the steps, and as he did so, the door opened and a uniformed figure loomed into view.

'Hullo!' said a gruff voice resembling the unloading of a ton of coal into an iron tank. 'Is that Inspector Evens?'

Evens hoisted himself out of the ton-neau and approached the steps. 'How d'ye do, Phillips?' he growled. 'Got your message and came straight on. This is Professor Barrington,' he added as the scientist and Hertford came up. 'You remember he helped us in the Wolverton case.'

Sergeant Phillips saluted. 'Pleased to meet you, sir,' he said, turning to Barrington. 'This is a strange business, a very strange business. Perhaps we'd better go inside.'

He led the way into the hall, and the others followed. Eustace Barrington glanced round with eyes keen on taking in every detail.

The inside of the house presented the same air of neglect as the grounds. The place was in the utmost disorder, and looked more like a sale-room at Christie's than a private residence. It was littered with curios from all countries and parts of the world. A mummy case from some Egyptian tomb stood cheek by jowl with an ivory idol of Chinese workmanship, while thrust carelessly into the hall-stand was a collection of Japanese swords and

South African spears. Propped up against the wall in one corner was a suit of Chinese armour which appeared about to collapse at any moment, beside which stood a packing-case overflowing with shavings, which strewed the floor in all directions. Over everything was a thick layer of dust, the accumulation of months, and the atmosphere held a strange nauseating smell of decay intermingled with the pungent odour of bitumen.

'Pretty dismal place, isn't it?' boomed Sergeant Phillips as he caught the expression on Hertford's face.

He opened a door on the left and signed to the others to enter. The room was fitted up as a half library, half study, and extraordinarily untidy. From the shelves which covered the walls, books overflowed and rioted across the floor, piling themselves in little heaps on chairs, tables, and every available corner. In the centre stood a large carved oak writing table strewn and littered with papers and a heterogeneous collection of objects which included ivory statuettes, curiously carved caskets, and several old pipes. One side had been cleared, and the remains of a meal, with a half-emptied bottle of Bass, struck an incongruous note amid the curios and ancient relics which overflowed the room in all directions.

By the side of a large armchair, on which lay an open book, was the body of a middle-aged man. He was dressed in an old dressing-gown, torn and discoloured. His neck was bare and collarless, and protruding from his breast was the handle of a knife.

'Nothing has been touched,' said Phillips. 'I thought that — '

'Who made the discovery?' interposed Eustace Barrington.

'Watts,' answered Phillips. 'He's a sort of general help from what I can gather. Lessard apparently didn't keep any servants, and wouldn't allow a woman about the place. But this fellow Watts used to come in every day and do odd jobs, and any cooking that was needed.'

'Where is Watts?' asked Barrington.

'In the kitchen. He seems to have had a great regard for his master, and is all knocked up over his death.'

'I should like to see him,' said

Barrington quietly.

The sergeant opened the door and his deep voice went booming over the house. In answer to his call, a little shrivelled man appeared and hesitated nervously on the threshold of the room. His face was thin and lined, and he possessed a shock of untidy flaring red hair that stuck out from his head in tufts, and which, coupled with an enormous hooked nose and tiny bead-like black eyes, gave him the appearance of a parrot. There was no mistaking that the man had received a severe shock. The traces of it were visible in every action.

'Now, Watts,' said Eustace Barrington kindly as he motioned the little man to a seat in the only chair in the room that was free from books, 'I want you to tell us how you first came to discover that your master had been killed.'

Watts moistened his lips and cleared his throat. 'Well, sir,' he began, 'I usually arrives here at about half past seven to get the breakfast ready, but this morning I was a bit late, and it must have been nearer eight. As I was comin' up the drive, I saw there was a light in this here room. You can see the winder from the drive before yer turns the corner what leads to the house. It didn't surprise me, much, 'cos the master was a rare one for gettin' up early, and very often he didn't go to bed at all, but sat up readin' all night.' He gulped slightly, but managed to go on.

'When I let myself in, I came straight to this here room, expectin' to find him sittin' at his table as usual. Then I seed him on the floor. At first I thought he had been took ill, but when I had another look and saw the knife in his chest, I realised what had happened.' He passed his tongue over his dry lips and tried to swallow the sob that rose in his throat.

'What did you do then?' asked the professor.

'Well, at first,' continued Watts, 'I was too upset to do anythin'. It fair struck me all of a heap, as yer might say. But after a bit I recovered myself and phoned the police station, and then the sergeant arrived, and that's all I know.'

'Have you known Lessard long, my

man?' said Inspector Evens.

'Nigh on twelve year. I was his batman when he was in the army.'

'You said just now,' said the scientist, 'that as soon as you saw the knife, you realized what had occurred. Did you have any cause to expect that anything like this might happen to your master?'

The little man hesitated and ran his fingers through his shock of hair. The professor repeated his question. 'Well, I can't say as how I expected it,' said Watts hesitatingly, 'but of late years the master had seemed as though he was nervous of somethin' or other.'

'In what way?' questioned Barrington.

'He was always enquirin' if I'd seen anyone hangin' round the place, and he seemed sort o' waitin' like for somethin' to happen. He got worse just lately, and he was thinkin' of gettin' me to come and stop here permanent, and bring my wife, because he said it was a lonely sort of a place and he didn't like bein' by himself at night.'

Barrington shot a quick glance at Evens, who was thoughtfully rubbing his bristling moustache with a stubby forefinger.

'When did he first seem nervous, as you call it?' asked the scientist.

'About three years ago,' answered the little man, 'just after he'd come back from his last explorin' trip. It was about a month after that.'

'Have you ever seen any suspicious-looking characters about?' interposed Evens.

'No, sir, I ain't,' said Watts, scratching his head. 'Until I came in this mornin' and found him — ' He nodded in the direction of the body. ' — I thought it was all his imagination. Sort o' nerves with livin' in this miserable hole, as yer might say.'

'And you don't know anything else that would be likely to help us?' queried Barrington. Watts shook his head. 'I don't think we need detain him any longer, Evens,' said the professor as he crossed over to the body and stood thoughtfully surveying it.

'Can I go then, sir?' asked Watts eagerly, looking from one to the other. 'If you don't want me anymore, I should like to go home to the wife.'

Detective Inspector Evens nodded shortly, and the little man scuttled to the door like a frightened rabbit, and they heard his footsteps as he ran down the steps from the front door.

'You see, Evens,' said the professor quietly as he rose from an examination of the body, 'the features are identical in both crimes, and I'm prepared to swear that the same hand is responsible. The murderer must have worked quickly, for after the killing of James Lessard on the Albert Embankment, he must have made his way straight down here.'

He commenced a close examination of the room, peering into corners, and lifting books and curios; subjecting everything to the closest scrutiny, his eyes darting hither and thither, so that not a speck of dust escaped their keen glances. Evens, his bulky black notebook in his hand, was noting down a resumé of the case.

At last Barrington finished his search. 'There's one detail about this second murder in which it differs from the first,' he said as he dusted the knees of his trousers.

'What's that, sir?' asked Hertford. Then, as he suddenly grasped the point that Barrington was driving at, 'You mean the tooth?'

'Yes,' said the scientist quietly. 'In the first case, the tooth was found beside the body, but in this instance there's not a trace of it.'

'Then the murderer must have taken it away with him,' said Hertford in astonishment.

'Exactly. And that starts a very interesting — '

'But in the name of sense,' broke in Evens, 'what for?'

'That's precisely what we've got to find out, my dear Evens,' murmured Barrington, his dark eyes alight with intense interest. 'To my mind, the whole solution of the mystery rests upon the apparently senseless connection, on the part of the murderer, in drawing the left canine teeth of his two victims. He must have possessed some strong motive. In my opinion, it was the motive for both these crimes.'

'But it's absurd,' snorted the Scotland Yard man. 'What possible reason could he have in wanting the teeth?'

'Tooth, Evens,' corrected Eustace Barrington. 'Don't forget that in the first instance he left the tooth behind him. Also, the knife used in this case — ' He pointed to the hilt protruding from the dead man's breast. ' — differs considerably from the knife used in the first crime. I should say that it had been taken from that collection of weapons on the wall in the hall. There was a vacant space, I remember. That point is worth considering . . . By the way,' he added, turning to Sergeant Phillips, 'have you discovered how the murderer gained access to the house?'

'Through a small window in the pantry,' answered Phillips. 'I'll show you.'

They followed him along the hall. At the end was a short flight of steps leading down into a spacious kitchen. Here a certain amount of order was discernible. Crossing the kitchen, Sergeant Phillips led the way to a small door at the other end, and opening it, disclosed to view a tiny room fitted as a pantry. At one end was a window, the hasp of which hung loose, the screw torn half out. The window was unbarred, and it would have been quite easy for anyone to have inserted some form of lever between the sash and forced the window back on its hinges. This was what apparently had been done.

Eustace Barrington examined the hasp and also the floor beneath the window. The hard cement with which the place was paved yielded nothing in the way of traces; and as it was obvious that this had been the mode of ingress, the scientist wasted little time.

'What does this window overlook?' he enquired.

'A small footpath leading round to the main drive,' replied Phillips.

Barrington opened the window wide and hoisted himself on to the sill. Pausing for a second to get his balance, he launched himself out onto the path. The force of his spring carried him a good four feet away from the window, and he landed on the grassy border which ran down one side of the narrow pathway. It was dark by now, and taking a torch from his pocket, which he never omitted to bring on these occasions, Barrington directed its powerful white beams on the path at his feet. He had purposely avoided jumping on the path in order not to obliterate any traces that might possibly be there, and now, as the rays of the powerful torch illumined the damp ground, he saw distinctly under the window the mark of two sharply defined footprints. They had evidently been made by a pair of narrow pointed shoes that had been shod with rubber soles, for on the right shoe-print a portion of the rubber had broken away near the heel.

Taking a slip of paper from his breast pocket, Barrington quickly made a tracing of the prints, and slipped it back into his pocket. Keeping on the grassy border, he moved on down the path, directing his light on the ground beside him as he walked. The footprints were plainly visible, leading down in the direction of the drive. But at the point where the path intersected the drive, they vanished into the tangle of weeds and brambles which bordered it, and all trace of them was lost.

The professor made his way to the front of the house, and as he ascended the steps he was met by Evens and Hertford. Briefly he informed them of his discoveries as they returned to the room of death.

Phillips was talking to a young constable who had arrived. The remains of James Lessard had been covered with a sheet and laid on a sofa, awaiting the arrival of the ambulance to take them to the infirmary. Evens gave orders for plaster casts to be made of the footprints.

Barrington began a systematic search of the papers on the writing table, in much the same way as he examined and classified germs. Nothing of importance rewarded his trouble, however, and he was in the act of finishing his investigations when a slip of paper which had been used as a bookmark attracted his attention.

It appeared to be part of a torn letter, and merely consisted of the letters S T R O, scrawled in ink. The rest had evidently belonged to the original from which this had been torn off.

For some minutes Eustace Barrington stared at this thoughtfully, his long slim fingers gently twisting his ring. Then he gave a sudden exclamation, and into the dark luminous eyes leapt a swift gleam of interest.

'What is it, sir?' cried Hertford, who had been watching him.

'It's a — ' began Barrington, but he broke off as a cry from Evens made him swing round.

'Look, Barrington! Look!' yelled the Scotland Yard man, gazing at the window.

They stared at the direction in which he pointed. The blind was only half drawn, and out of the darkness, pressed close against the glass of the window-pane, a white face looked in at them!

4

The Woman in the Grey Costume

Even as Evens yelled out, the face disappeared. With a quick spring, Eustace Harrington, with Hertford at his heels, was at the door, and in less than a second had torn it open and dashed from the hall. Flinging open the front door, the scientist raced down the steps and out onto the drive. Here he paused for a second, listening. Everything was silent. Suddenly Hertford gave a cry.

'There he is, Professor!' he shouted.

Barrington's eyes followed the direction in which his secretary was pointing. In a clearing in the thick trees which bordered the drive, he glimpsed for a second a shadowy figure which was making in the direction of the main road.

Like an arrow released from a bow, the professor was off in pursuit, closely followed by Hertford. Forcing their way through the tangled undergrowth of weeds and brambles, they hurried in the direction of the clearing where they had seen the figure.

'There he is again,' cried Hertford through his teeth as he raced along by Barrington's side. Suddenly out of the darkness ahead came the sharp crack of an automatic, and Hertford drew his breath with a hiss as a bullet whizzed past his head.

Crack! Again the sharp retort shattered the silence.

Barrington, his face white and tense, redoubled his efforts. There was no longer any sight of the intruder, and after those two shots everything was silent. They had passed the clearing by now, and the thickly planted trees made running at any pace next to impossible. All sign of the mysterious prowler had vanished, and presently, as they emerged by the broken fence which divided the grounds of Copthorn House from the roadway, Barrington was forced to give up all hope of coming to grips with his quarry. With a rueful smile, he turned to his secretary.

'I'm afraid we shall have to give it up, Bobbie,' he panted. 'It's impossible to trace anyone in this infernal wood. He must have doubled back after that last shot and gone off in another direction.' Slowly they started on their way back to the house. Inspector Evens, his face more red than usual with excitement, was standing at the bottom of the steps. He lumbered towards them as they emerged from the trees. 'Did you get him, Professor?' he puffed. 'I heard the shots, and — '

The scientist shook his head.

'I'm blowed if I know what to make of it all,' snorted the worthy inspector. 'If it was the chap who murdered Lessard, what in the world is he doing hanging round here?'

Barrington smiled. 'I don't think the answer to that is very hard to find,' he murmured, 'and I doubt very much if we've seen the last of him.'

'Why, sir,' cried Hertford, in amazement, 'you surely don't think he'll come back?'

'I think it extremely probable, Hertford,' answered the scientist. 'It was quite an error of judgment on his part to allow himself to have been seen just now.'

'Look here, Barrington,' burst out Evens excitedly, 'what are you getting at? Anyone 'ud think you were in private communication with the beggar, and knew exactly what he was going to do next.'

'No, no, my dear Evens,' said the professor, the ghost of a smile lifting the corners of his thin, firm, set mouth. 'I'm merely stating what I think to be a probability.'

Evens grunted. 'Well,' he said, 'I don't think there is any more to be done here. We might as well be getting back to town.'

He turned as he spoke, and started to ascend the steps. At that moment, from along the drive came the sharp tapping of running feet. The three swung round and faced the darkness as the hurrying steps drew nearer and nearer. Then out of the darkness burst a breathless running figure. As it drew nearer, Hertford gave a cry of astonishment. It was the figure of a woman!

As she caught sight of them in the light from the open door, she gave a little cry, and Eustace Barrington had barely time to spring forward as she crumpled up and collapsed in his arms in a dead faint!

Lifting her slight form in his arms, the scientist carried her into the house and placed her gently in the armchair, turning it so that it had its back to the silent figure on the couch.

At the professor's command, the young constable who had stood by, his eyes starting from his head with astonishment, went in search of water, while the scientist started chafing the hands of the woman.

She was quite young, certainly not more than twenty-one or -two, and exceedingly pretty. Hertford had removed her little close-fitting hat, and her head, covered with curling fair hair, formed a subject fit for an artist as it was thrown into relief against the dark upholstery of the chair. Her face was deadly pale, and there were dark blue shadows under the closed eyes. She was dressed in a beautifully fitting tailor-made costume of some smooth grey cloth resembling cashmere, and wore light stockings of the thinnest silk, which, together with the little high-heeled grey suede shoes, were spattered and splashed all over with mud.

Detective Inspector Evens stood looking down at her, and repeatedly running his fingers through his bristling hair.

'What in the world is she doing here, Professor?' he asked in bewilderment. 'Who is she?'

'My dear Evens,' replied Barrington impatiently as he loosened the high collar of her blouse at the throat, 'how the deuce should I know who she is? Possibly she will tell us with her own lips when she recovers.'

The constable returned at this moment with a glass of water. Eustace Barrington gently forced a few drops of the ice-cold liquid between the woman's parted lips, and wetting his handkerchief, dabbed her forehead. After a few minutes, a long fluttering sigh shook her, and her eyes slowly opened.

For a second she remained motionless. Then as consciousness fully returned, she started up with an articulate cry and gazed wildly round her in evident terror.

'Where — where am I?' she managed to gasp.

'Don't worry, little lady,' answered Barrington soothingly. 'You're quite safe, I assure you.'

'But — but,' she stammered, and raised her hand to her head, 'I must have fainted. It was terrible. I was so frightened. Out there in the dark!' She broke off, shuddering violently.

'What frightened you?' asked Barrington gently.

'The man I — who are you?' she asked, a strange look in her eyes.

'My name is Barrington — Eustace Barrington,' replied the scientist.

'Eustace Barrington!' she breathed. 'Not — not the famous scientist?'

'I certainly am a scientist,' he answered with a faint smile, 'but — '

'But what is this place?' she questioned as her eyes lighted on Inspector Evens and Bobbie Hertford, and from thence to the constable and Sergeant Phillips, who stood by the door. 'Is it a police station?'

Barrington laughed. 'No,' he replied, 'this is Copthorn House.'

The effect of his quietly spoken words was magical. The woman stared at him as though stung by some venomous serpent. The colour receded even from her lips, leaving them white and bloodless, while her large blue eyes opened wide, and into their depths came such an expression of terror as Barrington had seldom seen before in any human being. She half rose from her chair and stood, swaying giddily.

Thinking she was going to faint again, the professor stepped quickly forward, but she recovered herself by a supreme effort and waved him away. As she did so, her eyes, which were travelling round the room, lighted on the couch with its grim occupant. They heard the whistle of her breath as she drew it sharply inwards.

The professor stood motionless, watching her. Slowly she raised her hands to her eyes as though to shut out what she saw.

'What — what's that?' The words were scarcely audible, and her voice sounded hoarse and cracked, as though all moisture in her throat had suddenly dried up, as she asked the question.

Barrington took her by the arm and gently turned her round, away from the couch. As he did so, she suddenly sank back into the chair and burst into a fit of sobbing. He leaned down and gently patted her on the shoulder.

'Come, come,' he said, a, world of kindness in his voice, 'you mustn't go on like this. There's nothing to be afraid of. You're quite safe.'

She stifled her sobs and presently sat up, dabbing at her eyes with a wisp of lace handkerchief which she took from her bag.

'You're very kind,' she murmured gratefully as the scientist took out his flask and poured a few drops of brandy between her trembling lips. 'But if you knew how frightened I was — ' She broke off and laid a slender hand on his arm. 'Tell me,' she asked brokenly, 'what's happened here, and — ' She half looked round behind her. ' — who is that on the couch?'

Barrington hesitated, and Inspector Evens, who had been fidgeting impatiently for some time, broke in.

'I can't see exactly, miss,' he said gruffly, 'what concern it is of yours. But I should like you to account for your presence here. As to what has happened, it's a question of murder.'

'Murder!' The woman breathed the ominous word, and her hand contracted on Barrington's arm. 'Who — ' she continued in a voice that vibrated with suppressed emotion, 'who was it?'

'The owner of the house, James Lessard,' Barrington interposed quietly before Evens could reply.

'James Lessard,' repeated the woman in a low voice. 'Oh, how dreadful!'

'Now, miss,' said Inspector Evens, 'I should like to know who you are, and what you're doing here.'

The woman looked at him steadily for a moment or two before she answered. Then: 'I have every right here,' came the amazing reply. 'I'm Mrs. James Lessard.'

5

The Figure in the Wood

If a bombshell had suddenly exploded in their midst, it could not have created greater consternation. Detective Inspector Evens stared at the woman with his mouth open, a look of foolish amazement on his large red face, while Sergeant Phillips appeared no less astonished. Hertford was obviously taken aback at her quietly spoken assertion. Only Eustace Barrington remained outwardly unmoved. His face, with its tense eyes, remained expressionless, and not a trace of the thoughts that were running through his brain showed itself on his face.

For more than a minute no one spoke, and then Barrington broke the silence. 'I had no idea,' he said quietly to the woman, 'that James Lessard was married.'

She looked at him, a peculiar half-wistful smile playing about the corners of her well-shaped mouth. 'No — no one had,' she replied in a low voice. 'It was quite a secret. He didn't want it known.'

'Then you had no idea your husband had been killed?' asked Evens stupidly.

'No,' she replied. 'I haven't seen him for nearly three years.' She gave a little shiver, as if the recollection of the last time she had seen him conjured up in her mind some unpleasant memory.

'What brought you here tonight?' asked Barrington.

She fumbled in her bag before answering, and presently drew forth a piece of paper. 'I received this telegram this morning.' She held out the paper, and the professor took it.

'Moira Brennan, 27, Merrion Road, Liverpool,' it read. 'It is urgent that I should see you. Come at once, Copthorn House, Reigate. — LESSARD.'

Barrington passed it across to Inspector Evens. 'Sent at 9.30 last night,' he murmured, 'possibly over the phone, but too late to be received in Liverpool until this morning. Brennan, I presume,' he continued to the woman, 'is your maiden name?'

She nodded, and was about to speak when there came the sound of wheels on the drive outside, followed almost immediately by a thunderous knock at the front door.

'I expect that's the ambulance,' boomed Phillips as the constable went to answer the summons. He proved correct, and in a few moments all that remained of James Lessard was borne out and placed in the ambulance, and they heard the noise of the motor fade away in the stillness of the night, on its way to the mortuary.

It seemed as if the removal of the grim occupant of the couch had lifted a curtain of gloom from about the room. Barrington glanced at his watch; the hands pointed to twenty minutes to eight. Then he turned to Bobbie Hertford.

'If I remember rightly,' he said, 'there's a patch of dense shrubbery just by the foot of the steps on the other side of the drive. Will you slip out, Hertford, and run the car into the bushes, and conceal it as much as possible?'

Hertford looked rather surprised, but went away to carry out Barrington's instructions. Inspector Evens looked at the professor as if he had taken leave of his senses.

'I came to you for a little help, Professor,' he said, 'but it seems you've taken charge of the case.'

'Don't be annoyed, Evens,' he said quietly. 'I must work in my own way. You'll understand later. Now, Mrs. Lessard,' he continued, 'it's impossible for you to remain here all night, and it's equally impossible for you to venture out alone. I suggest that you return with us later to town, and we can then find accommodation for you at a hotel. In the meanwhile, perhaps you could tell us the circumstances under which you came to marry James Lessard, and the reason why it was kept such a profound secret. It may help to throw some light on the mystery surrounding his death.'

The woman looked up at him with troubled eyes. 'Must I?' she asked plaintively.

'In any case,' said Harrington gently, 'you'll have to give evidence at the inquest, and the whole story is bound to come out then. On the other hand, the facts may have a vital bearing on the case, and the delay give the criminal a chance of escape.'

He stepped over to the window and drew across the heavy curtains, arranging them so that not a ray of light could penetrate outside. Having done this to his satisfaction, he returned and seated himself opposite the woman. Inspector Evens, with a resigned shrug of his shoulders, cleared a pile of books from a chair by the simple expedient of tipping them on the floor, and settled his bulky form as comfortably as possible.

Hertford came back at that moment. The professor called him over and said something in a low tone, and he nodded and slipped out again.

'Now, Mrs. Lessard,' said the scientist.

'I hardly know where to begin,' she said hesitatingly, her eyes fixed on the floor as if seeking inspiration.

'Perhaps you'd better tell us everything,' suggested Barrington. 'How you became acquainted with James Lessard, and anything that suggests itself to you as likely to have any bearing on the matter.'

For a little while she remained silent; and then in a low voice, which grew louder as she went on, she began: 'James Lessard was a friend of my father's, and for many years, ever since I can remember, was in the habit of periodically turning up on a visit to our house, which lasted sometimes for a week, sometimes longer, and often perhaps not longer than two or three days.

'I believe they'd known each other all their lives. My father was a lonely man, and beyond Mr. Lessard, I don't think he possessed any other intimate friends at all.

'My mother died shortly after I was born, and my father never really recovered from the shock of her death.' She paused for a moment, and then went on: 'My father was a dental surgeon, and I believe his practice was a fairly prosperous one. I know that he had a large number of patients, so many, in fact, that he was forced to employ an assistant. I could never stand the man, Paul Harte, although I believe he was very capable. Indeed, father used to say that he was a great deal cleverer than he was.

'However, there was something about him — what it was, I couldn't exactly define — that made me distrust him. One night, a little more than three years ago, Mr. Lessard — I can never really think of him as anything else — arrived at our house on one of his periodical visits. I remember it was just as we were sitting down to dinner.

'He seemed strangely excited, and although he talked throughout the meal about his travels, and various other subjects, as usual, his mind appeared to be fixed upon something else, and he seemed to welcome the time when dinner was over. He made a remark once that was unusual. He told my father that he would like him to have a look at his teeth. I know it struck me at the time that it was a strange thing for him to say, because my father had always said what a wonderful set of teeth Mr. Lessard had, and that if everyone's teeth were as good as his, all the dentists in the world would go bankrupt.

'As soon as dinner was finished, he

carted my father off to the surgery. Paul Harte offered to accompany them, but Mr. Lessard made some laughing remark that he would prefer Father to do the examination, as being a friend of his, he probably wouldn't hurt him so much.

'They didn't appear again that evening, but as I passed the surgery door on the way to the kitchen to give some final instructions to the servants before going to bed, I heard them talking excitedly, and Mr. Lessard's voice say, 'It's impossible to be too careful . . . divide it. It means thousands . . . the best place to conceal . . . ' He lowered his voice, and I didn't catch the rest of what he was saying.

'On my return from the kitchen, I ran up against Harte hanging about outside the surgery door. He was obviously taken aback at seeing me, and muttered something which I couldn't catch. He was plainly eavesdropping, and I determined to tell Father about it in the morning.

'My father was already at breakfast when I came down, but there was no sign of Mr. Lessard, and Father told me he had left early, as he had some business to transact in London. At the first opportunity, I told Father about Harte listening at the surgery door on the previous night, and he seemed very perturbed, and asked me if I'd heard anything. I told him what I'd heard Mr. Lessard say, and he made me promise that I'd never repeat it to anyone. And until now, I never have. Whether he said anything to Harte, I don't know, but everything went on as usual for the next week, except that my father appeared to be ill at ease, and seemed to have something weighing on his mind.'

She stopped for a second and moistened her lips. Barrington's fingers sought and found his ring as he listened intently, while Inspector Evens had taken the familiar black notebook from his pocket and was jotting down notes every now and again as she proceeded.

'About a week must have elapsed,' she continued, 'when Mr. Lessard turned up again, and the same night my father followed me up to bed.

''Moira', he said, shutting the door

behind him, 'I've got something to say to you.' His voice was very grave. 'I've been feeling far from well lately, and owing to some unfortunate speculations, I'm not as well off as you imagine, and I'm worried as to what will become of you should anything happen to me. I've talked it over with Lessard, and it's my dearest wish that you and he should marry.'

'I was at first struck dumb with amazement. It was the last thing I had expected. 'But,' I began, when father raised his hand and stopped me.

''Don't misunderstand me, child,' he said. 'It need only be in name, and no one need be any the wiser. In fact, it's only on these conditions that Lessard will agree to the marriage at all. But it will relieve my mind of a lot of anxiety to know that you'll always be well looked after.'

'At first I refused, but I was very young, and my father pleaded so hard that eventually I consented; and at the end of the week Mr. Lessard and I were married quietly at the registry office. I shall never forget that morning as long as I live. Everything seemed like a nightmare, and but for the fact that Father seemed to be relieved, there was little or no pleasure about an event that should have been one of the greatest joys of my life.

'As we left the registrar's office, Mr. Lessard gently took my hand and removed the ring he'd slipped onto my finger during the ceremony, and put it in his pocket.

''There's now nothing to remind you of this,' he said quietly. My father had already taken charge of the certificate, which had been handed to me, and nothing more was ever said about the marriage. The following day my father went out for a walk in the evening, as was his usual habit, but he never came back; and from that day to this, nothing's been seen or heard of him! He completely disappeared! We informed the police, and the most searching enquiries were instituted, but all to no purpose. It was as if the ground had opened and swallowed him up!'

She choked back a little sob which had come into her throat, and it was some time before she recovered herself sufficiently to continue.

'During the ensuing days, Mr. Lessard

was kindness itself; no one could have been more considerate. The strain of my strange marriage and the worry of my father's mysterious disappearance had their effect, and for some days I was confined to bed with a severe nervous breakdown.

'My father, I discovered, was heavily in debt, and as week after week went by without any sign or news of him, I was compelled at last to sell the practice to pay his creditors. After that, I went to share a flat with an old school friend, and have lived there ever since.

'Mr. Lessard left directly after the practice was sold, but before he went away, he instructed me to communicate with his bankers if ever I wanted anything. He arranged to make me an allowance, which I received each month direct from his bank, and I never heard anything from him or saw him again until I received this telegram this morning.

'I caught the first available train to London, hoping that he might have received some news of my father. I enquired my way here from the station, and was walking up the road when I thought I saw a man lurking in the shadows. At first I thought it was my imagination, but after a time I became convinced that someone was following me.

'It frightened me, and I started to run. The man started to run, too, and I turned into the nearest gateway, never guessing that I'd arrived at my destination, and that it was Copthorn House.'

As she concluded, Eustace Harrington leaned forward in his chair. 'It's a most extraordinary story, Mrs. Lessard,' he said. 'And although it's put us in possession of some fresh facts, it does little to clear up the mystery surrounding your husband's death. In fact, it tends more to deepen it. I suppose you saw nothing which would enable you to identify the man who followed you up the road if you saw him again?'

'No,' she answered. 'It was too dark, and — '

At that moment, Hertford opened the door and entered the room. His eyes were shining with excitement. 'Quick sir,' he said, hurriedly. 'He's here again — over by the gap in the trees!'

Eustace Barrington, his face tense and alert, sprang to his feet. 'Come on, Evens!' he snapped. 'Don't make a sound! Wait here, Mrs. Lessard.'

He hurried quickly into the hall. It was in darkness, and the front door stood slightly open.

'Not a sound!' whispered the scientist. As swift and noiseless as a shadow, he slipped down the steps, his tall figure bent almost double.

To the right, away among the dense woodland which bordered the drive, a tiny light glowed among the trees. Hither and thither it darted, like an enormous firefly — twinkled — went out — and twinkled again — a ghostly will-o'-the-wisp dancing in the darkness of the night.

Barrington's hand closed for a second on Bobbie's arm, and they began to move forward, choosing that portion of the ground they were covering which was in the deepest shadow.

Suddenly Hertford halted. 'Light's gone out,' he breathed.

'Ssh,' hissed Barrington between his teeth as he continued to move forward in the direction where the light had been.

It was difficult moving among that tangle of undergrowth, and it was with difficulty that they avoided making any noise. The scientist was slightly in front, and as they paused for a moment in the pitch darkness to listen, they heard the faint sounds of someone moving ahead of them.

All at once the light flashed on again, and now they were near enough to distinguish that it came from an electric torch held in the hand of a shadowy figure dressed in black. The rays of the torch were directed on the ground, in a slight clearing among the trees, and the figure seemed to be searching for something. A piece of some dark material had been wrapped round the top of the torch so that only a tiny disc of light was visible.

Nearer and nearer crept Barrington and Hertford, and at last they reached the clearing. The secretary felt the professor's muscles tense, and as the figure in front bent down to examine a further patch of ground, the scientist sprang forward with a bound. In an instant, the figure in black dropped the torch and sprang away, but Barrington caught him round the waist. The man's strength was enormous, and he flung him off. Barrington's foot caught in a twisted root, and taken unawares, he went spinning headlong.

'Hold him, Hertford,' he shouted as he reeled backwards.

Hertford, a few yards behind, caught Barrington's shouted warning and darted forward, springing swiftly towards the man. But the fellow was even swifter! Dodging neatly to one side, he shot out a leg, and Bobbie, unable to check his own impulsive rush, tripped against it and crashed heavily to the ground.

Barrington was up now, and tearing in the direction where he could hear the fugitive crashing through the undergrowth. It was too dark to see clearly, and it was only by the sound the other made in his headlong flight that Barrington could detect in which direction he was travelling.

Suddenly, ahead, came a shout followed by a muttered curse, and a light flashed out. For a second it shone full on the fugitive, and the professor saw that his face was concealed by a dark handkerchief, so that only the eyes were visible between it and the brim of a soft hat.

'Heavens — you!' burst from the lips of the unknown. There was the sharp whip-like crack of an automatic, followed by the sound of a falling body, and the light went out!

Barrington dashed on breathlessly, and then suddenly he stumbled and almost fell. His foot had struck against something soft! Groping in the darkness, the professor felt about, and his searching fingers touched something warm. Searching in his pocket, he found his matchbox and struck a light. It was the body of a man! Before the match burnt out, Barrington found the torch by the still-outstretched hand, and pressing the catch, flooded the scene with light. Hertford came dashing up at the same moment, and together they surveyed the silent form.

The professor dropped on one knee beside the body. It was that of an elderly man, clean-shaven, whose face bore traces of recent illness. The professor laid his hand upon the breast.

'Quite dead!' he muttered. 'The bullet must have passed through the heart.'

'Who can he be?' asked Hertford in a hushed voice.

'I've no idea, Bobbie,' answered Barrington, and then suddenly he bent forward swiftly and directed the torch fully upon the dead man's face. The mouth was slightly open, and gently the scientist turned back the upper lip.

'Look!' was all he said, quietly, an expression of the utmost mystification on his face. Hertford gave a quick gasp as he bent forward.

The upper left canine tooth was missing, and it had been recently drawn!

At that moment, Inspector Evens burst through the shrubbery, puffing and panting, followed by Mrs. Lessard. 'Have you got him?' he asked.

Barrington signed to Bobbie to stop the woman from catching sight of the figure on the ground, but he was too late. The light was shining full upon the upturned face, and as her eyes rested upon it, she gave a sharp cry of recognition.

'Oh,' she cried, stepping forward. 'Oh, my God!'

'What's the matter, Mrs. Lessard?' said Barrington. 'Do you know this man?'

'Yes, yes,' she gasped, swaying dizzily. 'It's my father!' And she slipped to the ground in a dead faint.

6

Links in the Chain

In spite of the lateness of the hour at which he retired, Bobbie Hertford was up early the next morning. It was the custom of Professor Barrington to do a certain amount of work on his new treatise before breakfast each day, and Hertford felt sure that not even the exciting events of the previous night would keep him from it. Barrington possessed the strange faculty of shutting one thing entirely out of his mind and concentrating on something else of a vastly different nature.

On his way down he met the housekeeper, Mrs. Timpson, who had been in Barrington's service for more than a quarter of a century, and was a valued servant. It was an unusually early hour for her to be about. 'Good morning, Mrs. Timpson,' Bobbie said. 'Is the professor in his study?'

'Yes, sir.' She smiled at Hertford as she

spoke, for he was a great favourite with the servants. 'That's why I'm up so early this morning. I heard you both come in last night, Mr. Hertford, and I heard you go to bed; but although I listened for some time, I didn't hear the master come up. When I woke up this morning, I felt sure he was still in the study. I'm a very light sleeper, Mr. Bobbie, and I'm sure I should have wakened up if he had come upstairs.'

Bobbie whistled. 'An unusual thing for the professor to do. But the fact is, something of great interest to him happened yesterday — a rather unusual crime; and as you know, the solving of crimes is his great hobby. I've never known him to sit up all night over one until now, though. Perhaps I'd better see if he wants me, and will you send a maid up with some coffee, please?'

Arriving at the door of the study, Hertford opened it gently and looked in. The professor was pacing the room with a slow measured tread as though his steps were keeping time to the rhythm of his thoughts. The intense dark eyes, deep set in the frame of his massive head, seemed to be piercing into the unknown as though only there could be a solution found. He was weighing up all the facts of the case carefully, selecting those which were of value and discarding others which he considered unimportant; his keen scientific brain building up theory after theory until eventually the whole problem would resolve itself clearly before his mind, emerging from a heterogeneous collection of seemingly unconnected incidents and events, and gradually assuming a connected whole, as one would build up the picture of a jigsaw puzzle from the scattered fragments before him.

The fingers of his right hand still twisted the ring round and round the finger of his left hand. It seemed like some ancient talisman that might at any moment yield up its secret power and give the answer to the riddle that was harassing the professor's mind.

After the astounding discovery of the dead body of Mrs. Lessard's father in the grounds of Copthorn House, shot down before their very eyes, and the subsequent escape of the unknown prowler, Barrington and Inspector Evens had carried the unconscious woman back into the house, where they had succeeded in bringing her round. After the first terrible shock had worn off, she grew calm, although plainly heartbroken at the discovery. At the same time, a merciful numbness of her faculties had mitigated the blow to a great extent.

The necessary formalities demanded by the law having been complied with, and Detective Inspector Evens having given Sergeant Phillips his parting instructions, Barrington's car had been recovered from its place of concealment in the bushes, and the little party of four had started for London. Barrington had slipped away for a few minutes just before they started, and when he returned, Hertford noted that there was an expression of quiet satisfaction on the professor's mobile face.

On their arrival in London, Barrington's first care had been the woman, and he had secured accommodation for her at a quiet private hotel near Welbeck Street, the proprietress of which, an elderly motherly woman, was well known to the professor.

Briefly he informed her of the circumstances, and gave Mrs. Lessard into her charge with instructions to look after her.

Inspector Evens had gone on to Scotland Yard to make his report, and Barrington and his secretary, after garaging the car, made their way home to Welbeck Street, They had eaten nothing all that day, and were glad of the substantial supper which Mrs. Timpson had laid in the study, although Hertford was almost too tired to do justice to the meal. After Bobbie had gone to bed, Barrington, in an unusually perturbed frame of mind, had decided to go over the facts of the case whilst they were still fresh in his mind.

Hour succeeded hour, and still he paced the room, twisting the ring now this way, now that, his thoughts concentrating on the problem before his mind, oblivious alike of time and place.

That the same hand was responsible for all three murders he had no doubt whatever. The fact that in each case the victim had been deprived of his left canine tooth stamped the crimes as the work of one man, or if more than one, a combination working together with one definite purpose in view.

In the case of the murder of Brennan, Moira Lessard's father, the tooth had certainly been removed some considerable time before his death. The detective had ascertained that when he had examined the man's mouth, but at the most it had not been more than two or three days before, as the condition of the gums proved.

According to Mrs. Lessard's story, her father had disappeared nearly three years previously. Where had he been in the meantime, and what had induced him to absent himself for so long a period? And why had he turned up at Copthorn House on the very day that his friend, Lessard, had been murdered?

Some secret evidently had been shared between himself and Lessard, a secret which apparently presented a certain element of danger to both of them. What was this mystery? Then again, there was the man on the Embankment. How did he fit into the puzzle? Was he any relation of Lessard's, or was the fact that his name was the same merely a coincidence? In his case, the tooth had been found beside him on the Embankment. And then there was the mysterious night prowler at Copthorn House who wore a mask to conceal his face. Who was he? He must have been intimately connected with Moira Lessard's father, for on the instant before he had shot him, he had uttered that cry of recognition, 'Heavens — you!', and he must have killed him to prevent Brennan talking, and incriminating him.

In that case, the old man must have known who he was. Could he have been the same man who had followed Moira Lessard up the road? And, if so, for what reason did he risk the danger of arrest by remaining hanging about Copthorn House?

A smile played for a second around the professor's mobile mouth. The answer to that, he believed, reposed at that moment in one of his waistcoat pockets. A vague idea had formed itself in Barrington's brain, an idea so fantastic that for a moment he hardly allowed himself to give it credence. It was at that time but a shadowy thing, but it more or less fitted the facts. He felt convinced that the hub of the whole mystery lay in the apparently meaningless and senseless action on the part of the murderer in extricating the canine tooth from each of his victims. And old Brennan, Moira Lessard's father, had been a dental surgeon! Surely that was more than a coincidence.

As the night wore on, the idea grew, took shape and became coherent. The only link in the chain of the scientist's reasoning which would not fit was the first James Lessard — the man on the Embankment. What had he been doing there, in the fog, at that hour of the morning? Harrington had made certain that he had walked down the Embankment from the Westminster end, for on the soles of his shoes he had discovered traces of fresh cement where he had passed over the spot where the workmen had been relaying the pavement. But it was hardly likely that any man in his senses would choose to walk down the Albert Embankment at half past twelve on a cold, raw, foggy morning for amusement. Something must have brought him there. What?

The first grey streaks of dawn had given

way to pale sunlight, and still the scientist sat on, lost in thought. As Hertford opened the door of the study, he suddenly twisted round his feet with a little exclamation of triumph.

'Good morning, Hertford! Ready for work?' he said, his eyes twinkling for a moment.

'Yes, sir, quite ready,' Hertford replied, 'but not feeling quite as spruce as usual.'

'Then suppose we leave it for a moment. The fact is, Hertford,' he went on, 'I've seldom been so intrigued by a crime mystery before or met with one that's held my attention in this way.'

He went to the window and flung up the sash, and the cool sweet air of the morning poured into the room.

After a hot bath and a good breakfast, Barrington felt as fit as a fiddle, and none the worse for his all-night sitting. Just as they finished the meal, the telephone rang sharply.

'See who it is, Bobbie,' said Barrington as he seated himself at his desk and started opening the morning mail. Hertford picked up the receiver.

'It's Evens, sir,' said the secretary a moment later. 'He wants to speak to you.'

The scientist took the telephone from Hertford's hand. Over the wire came the gruff voice of Inspector Evens.

'Good morning, Professor,' he said, 'I thought I'd just ring up and let you know that in answer to our enquiries, we've discovered that the James Lessard found on the Embankment is no relation to Lessard the explorer. He's quite well known, though, at his club, and appears to have been a fairly easy-going bachelor, not rich, but quite well off. Everyone who knew him appears to have liked him, and there seems to be no reason at all that accounts for his death. I've discovered why he was on the Embankment, though — found it at his flat. It only tends to deepen the mystery, if anything. It's a note, apparently from a woman signing herself Winfred, and implored him to meet her on the Albert Embankment between twelve and twelve thirty.'

'No address, of course,' said Barrington.

'No. It's written on half a sheet of paper from an ordinary cheap writing block, in pencil, and was delivered at Lessard's club by a district messenger — the porter remembers the envelope — about four thirty in the afternoon. We're trying to trace the boy; Sergeant Wilson's looking after that. I'm coming right away, Professor, and I'll bring the letter with me.'

He rang off. The professor hung up the receiver and sat for some time staring thoughtfully in front of him. Hertford was standing over by the window, gazing down at the stream of traffic in Welbeck Street. Suddenly he turned round.

'How did you know that the man who was prowling about Copthorn House last night would come back a second time, sir?' he asked curiously.

The scientist looked up, smiling slightly. 'I thought it very probable that he would,' he answered. 'That's why I told you to put the light out in the hall and watch for him. With the house apparently in darkness, and the car gone, he concluded, as I hoped he would, that we had departed, and he was free to continue his interrupted search.'

Hertford turned a look of keen surprise

and inquiry on the professor. 'Search, sir?' the secretary exclaimed. 'Do you think he was looking for something?'

'I'm certain he was,' replied the scientist quietly.

'But what could he have been looking for?' asked Bobbie in bewilderment.

'I have an idea he was looking for this.' Barrington put his hand into his waistcoat pocket and held a small object up between his long forefinger and thumb.

Hertford's eyes widened in amazement and wonder. It was a tooth! 'Where did you get it from, Professor?' he asked.

'You remember when I left you for a few minutes, before we started home,' said Barrington, twisting the tooth about in his steady, capable fingers, 'I went back to the place where I'd seen the man searching, and it wasn't long before I found this. I expected to find it. It had dropped into a little hollow formed by the interlacing roots of two trees. I expect that's why our friend the prowler overlooked it. A few feet away was the mark of an open hand on the ground, and I conclude that in his hurried flight, after killing Lessard and extracting the tooth, he tripped and fell, the tooth flying from his hand as he did so.'

'But — but,' gasped Hertford, a baffled look in his eyes, 'what does it all mean? Why should he take all this trouble, and run such a risk, for the sake of a tooth?'

'He committed murder to get the tooth,' answered Barrington quietly.

'You think the tooth was the motive for the crime?' asked Hertford.

Barrington nodded, and briefly he outlined to his secretary Mrs. Lessard's curious story, while Bobbie listened with rapt attention.

'It's got me beaten, sir!' he exclaimed at last, when Barrington had concluded. 'What on earth is the meaning of it all? Why did Mrs. Lessard's father turn up at Copthorn House, and what in the world can the tooth — '

'I can't answer any of your questions now,' returned Barrington, 'for the very simple reason that I don't know myself — yet. Of course, the whole thing is capable of an explanation, but at the moment that explanation eludes me.

83

However, I have a faint idea in my mind, and I propose very shortly to put part of it, at least, to the test.'

He took out a powerful lens and closely examined the tooth, which he held in his hand. There was a puzzled frown on his face as he did so. For nearly five minutes he continued to study it, turning it this way and that. Hertford was simply aching to ask a string of questions, but he knew the professor of old. When the time was ripe for an explanation, Barrington would explain, as was his wont.

At that moment there was a ring at the doorbell, followed by the deep, gruff voice of Detective Inspector Evens as he wished the maid good morning.

'Ha, Professor!' he said, rather full of his own importance. 'I've brought round the letter I spoke about on the phone, and — ' He broke off as his eyes caught sight of the tooth in the scientist's hand. 'Why, what's that?'

'A tooth,' said Eustace Barrington quietly, smiling softly. Inspector Evens glared.

'I can see it's a tooth,' he snapped. 'But whose? Where did you get it?'

Barrington explained.

'You see, Evens,' he went on, 'although this tooth has not the slightest suggestion of decay, it has been, for some reason or other, stopped with gold. I propose now to remove the gold filling!'

Evens stared at him in astonishment. 'Look here,' Barrington,' he demanded, 'what are you getting at? If you think this is a joke — '

'You'll see what I'm getting at in a minute,' interposed the scientist. 'And I can assure you it's very far from a joke.'

He opened a drawer in his desk and took out a small case from which he produced a tiny file. Hertford and Evens gathered round him interestedly as he commenced work on the gold filling of the tooth. For some minutes he worked quickly, surely; Hertford watched, fascinated. He could not guess what was in the back of the professor's mind, but he suspected that Barrington was about to put a theory of his to the test.

Suddenly a low, almost inaudible sound escaped the scientist, and young Hertford saw that he had succeeded in removing the filling. Taking a pin from a tray on the desk, Barrington gently probed in the cavity from which the filling had been removed. After a second or two, a small dark object rolled out onto the desk. The scientist picked it up and placed it in the palm of his hand.

Evens and Hertford bent eagerly forward. In the professor's palm lay a small round steel ball, like a bullet, and irregularly over its surface projected tiny protuberances — five in all.

Eustace Barrington surveyed it in obvious perplexity. 'That caused the death of three men,' he remarked quietly.

7

Hertford Takes Up the Trail

'Well, I'm blest!' exclaimed Detective Inspector Evens when he had sufficiently recovered his breath to be able to speak at all. 'If that doesn't beat everything! What in the world is it, Professor?'

The scientist shrugged his shoulders and turned the little ball over and over with his finger. 'I haven't the least idea,' he declared candidly. 'What can be the meaning of it, or what it's intended for, I can't at the moment imagine. One thing, however, is certain. It must possess some extraordinary value to the person or persons who are after it, seeing as they don't hesitate to commit murder to obtain possession of it.'

'Is it solid, sir?' put in Hertford. 'Perhaps there's something inside.'

Barrington examined it through his lens.

'It appears to be quite solid, Bobbie,' he said at length. 'No, I don't think there can be anything concealed in it.'

'I said at the beginning that it was the most extraordinary case I'd ever come across,' snorted the worthy inspector, 'and, by Jove, I was right!' He pulled a large handkerchief from his pocket and blew his nose violently, as though to clear away the mists which seemed to surround his brain.

Eustace Barrington took a little box from a drawer in his desk, and putting the little ball and the remains of the tooth into it, slipped it into his pocket.

'May I see the letter?' he asked as Evens finished blowing his nose and put away his handkerchief. The inspector fumbled in his pocket and produced the bulky black notebook from its capacious depths. He withdrew an envelope and handed it to Barrington.

It was an ordinary cheap white envelope which could have been procured at any stationer's, and the address was roughly scrawled across in pencil. Barrington took out the single sheet of paper it contained. This was also of a cheap quality. Without any prefix, the letter began:

'I must see you. It is most important. Will you meet me on the Albert Embankment tonight between 12 and 12.30? Please don't let anything detain you, James. It is really urgent.

'WINIFRED.'

'You found this at his flat?' asked Barrington, looking up at Evens.

'On the dressing table,' was the inspector's answer. 'Lessard left the club at a quarter to six, to change, as he was dining with a friend and his wife at Victoria. Bolton — that's the man — is also a member of the club to which Lessard belonged; and after Lessard had changed, he came back to the club, and Bolton and he drove to Victoria together. Sergeant Wilson saw Bolton and got this information from him direct. Bolton also states that Lessard left his flat about eleven thirty. Owing to the fog, Bolton asked him to stop the night, but Lessard made some excuse and drove off in a taxi.'

'Presumably to keep his appointment with the woman,' said Barrington, 'since it would have taken him quite half an hour to have reached the Albert Embankment in that fog.'

'We shall probably get some clue to the sender of the letter when we've located the messenger who delivered it,' said the inspector. 'In the meantime, we seem to have reached a blank wall. The whole affair is absolutely baffling. As far as I can see, there appears to be no rhyme or reason in it. What do you make of it, Professor?'

Eustace Barrington smiled thoughtfully. 'It's a little too soon to answer that question, my dear Evens,' he replied. 'I certainly have got the germ of a vague theory, but at the moment it's too indefinite to put into words.'

Hertford had returned to his position by the window, and now he turned suddenly. 'Professor,' he said excitedly, 'I'm sure there's a man watching the house. Look!'

The scientist rose and crossed over to Bobbie's side. 'Be careful, my boy,' he warned, pulling Hertford to one side of the curtain. 'If there's someone watching, we don't want to let them have the slightest inkling that we're aware of the fact.'

'There he is,' said Hertford. 'Look on the opposite side of the street — by that lamp post! I'm positive he's watching this house. He's been there for some time. He was there when I looked out before. Just before you discovered the steel ball in the tooth.'

Eustace Barrington looked across the street, being careful to keep himself hidden behind the curtain. On the opposite side of the road, leaning up against a lamp post and reading a paper, was a shabbily dressed seedy-looking man. He wore a dilapidated mackintosh and a dirty brownish-grey felt hat drawn low down over his eyes. Every now and again he darted a quick look across the street, at the door of the scientist's house.

'I believe you're right, my boy,' said Barrington, and a quick gleam came into his dark eyes. 'But we've got to make sure.' He thought for a moment. 'If what I believe is correct,' he went on quickly, 'the man's interest is centred upon me! Therefore, if I should leave the house, he'll follow me — and if he does, we'll know that our suspicions are a certainty. Come on, Evens, we'll put it to the test.' The scientist rang for his hat and coat as he spoke.

'If he does follow us,' snapped Evens grimly, 'I can arrest him on suspicion, and — '

'No, no!' interposed Barrington. 'That would be a fatal mistake. There's no evidence to convict him of any crime, and you'd only have to let him go again. I want to find out who he is and where he comes from. As soon as we leave the house, Hertford,' he went on, turning to his secretary, 'I want you to watch from the window, and if our mysterious friend starts to follow us, slip out immediately and trail him in turn.'

Hertford's eyes sparkled. He had been longing for an opportunity to take an active part in the case, and had been feeling just a trifle fed up at his own inactivity. But here was a chance to really do something. Visions of exciting discoveries rose before his youthful enthusiastic mental gaze.

As Barrington and Inspector Evens left the room, Hertford took up his position by the window. A moment after, he heard the hall door open and shut; and the burly form of Inspector Evens, accompanied by the tall, impressive figure of Eustace Barrington, left the house and proceeded at a leisurely pace up Welbeck Street in a northerly direction.

Hertford waited, his eyes fixed on the man on the other side of the street. A moment passed, and then another, and still the man remained where he was against the lamp post. Bobbie's heart sank. Had he been mistaken after all? No! Suddenly, with a well simulated yawn, the man folded his paper and thrust it into the pocket of his greasy mackintosh, and moved off in the direction taken by the scientist and Inspector Evens.

Bobbie waited no longer. Grabbing his hat and coat and struggling into them, he bounded down the stairs, and pausing for a moment at the door, waited just long enough for his movements to be safe, and slipped out. A glance up the street, and he made out the figures of his employer and Evens in the distance, while behind them lounged the man who had been watching the house.

This hobby of crime detection had made both Hertford and Eustace Barrington masters in the art of shadowing. Strolling along Welbeck Street, apparently enjoying the winter sunshine, no one who saw Hertford would have imagined for one instant that he was engaged on anything more important than the gentle art of killing time; but not a solitary gesture of the man in front escaped his keen young eyes. At the top of Welbeck Street, Detective Inspector Evens hailed a taxi, and waving farewell to Barrington, drove off. The scientist stood for a moment at the edge of the pavement, and then continued northward.

The mysterious shadower still followed him, keeping on the other side of the street. On went Barrington, swinging along with an easy stride, and covering the ground at a fairly respectable pace. He made his way to the Marylebone Road, and just where it merged into the Eustace Road, he paused suddenly, and stepping into the road, sprang on to a passing bus heading for King's Cross.

Hertford chuckled to himself. Barrington was evidently out with the intention of leading the shadower a pretty dance. For a moment, the man seemed to be non-plussed, but at that instant an empty taxi rolled slowly down the road. The man hailed it, and giving a hurried direction to the driver, drove off in the wake of the bus boarded by the professor. Hertford looked hastily round for another taxi. There was not one in sight anywhere.

He wrinkled his brows in perplexity. 'This is where I lose the beggar if I'm not careful,' he muttered as he broke into a run. 'Confound the professor! What did he want to get on that bus for?'

The taxi was rapidly outdistancing him, and Hertford knew that in a little while it would have disappeared from his sight. To have to go back and inform Barrington that he had failed, that he had lost his quarry, was unthinkable. The very thought of it filled Bobbie's heart with chagrin. If only he could find a taxi. He paused, panting, and looked round. Then his heart gave a bound of relief.

Another bus was coming in his direction down the road. Hertford ran out into the roadway, and the bus slowed down to enable him to spring on board. He took his place inside, in a vacant seat at the front of the bus, from which he could command a view of the street ahead.

In front he could still discern the taxi, and a little further in front still, Barrington's bus. Hertford took a penny ticket, ready to jump off the instant he espied an empty taxi, for he had no idea how far the scientist was going. At King's Cross, however, Hertford's bus speeded up and drew up almost behind the one Barrington was on, and the secretary saw the tall figure of his employer, as the scientist slipped off the bus in front, and strode into the station.

Bobbie got out and looked round for the mysterious trailer. He was hurriedly paying the taxi driver, and a second later also entered the station, with Hertford following closely at his heels. Eustace Barrington was making for the underground railway, and the next moment was disappearing down the stairs leading to the booking offices. Mingling with the little crowd of people who were also bound for the same destination, the man in the greasy mackintosh kept close to the scientist's elbow. Barrington took a ticket to the Angel, asking for it in a particularly loud voice.

Hertford and the shadower followed suit, and the secretary was so close to the man that it was possible for him to get a clear view of his face. It was thin and long, and of a peculiar pasty yellow complexion; the mouth thin, and curled at the corner, gave a curiously lupine expression to the man's face; the eyes were large and deeply sunken, while from between them projected a thin curved nose. The perpetual snarl which played about the twisted mouth gave to the man's features an animal-like expression. Altogether, it was a cruel face. The sort of face which suggests that its owner stops at nothing to gain his own ends.

Barrington, disdaining the lift, was leisurely descending the stairs to the platform, lighting a cigar as he did so. The lift was about to start on its journey downwards, and the man in the mackintosh hesitated a moment between it and the stairs, finally making up his mind to take the lift, apparently with the intention of meeting the scientist at the bottom.

Hertford pushed his way in front of him, and they both succeeded in entering the lift just as the gates clanged to. As soon as they reached the bottom, the man hurried out and almost ran for the platform from which the trains started for the Angel. About five or six people were standing about, but there was no sign of the professor. Barrington had disappeared. For a second the man stood gazing up and down the platform, and then, whirling round on his heel, he dashed for the staircase leading to the street.

Taking three steps at a time, he bounded up, with Hertford well behind him. Bobbie took care to keep the curve of the staircase between himself and his quarry, for it would never do for the man to recognise him as being the same fellow who had descended with him in the lift. It would rouse his suspicions instantly. The fact that Eustace Barrington had neatly tricked him must have shown him that the scientist was aware that he was being followed, and if the shadower once suspected that he was being tracked in turn, then all hope of discovering who he was, and whence he came, would be gone. Barrington, with his keen brain, had presumably foreseen that having lost him, the man would in all probability make for home, thus enabling Hertford to run him to earth and discover his identity.

Arriving at the top of the stairs, the shadower stood gazing in all directions, but to no purpose. There was not a sign of Barrington anywhere.

For some time the man started walking up and down, darting glances hither and thither round him. At last, apparently making up his mind that he had lost his quarry for good, for that time at least, he suddenly started at a rapid pace for the exit to the station.

Where are we off to now, I wonder, thought Hertford as he followed along in the rear.

Apparently the man at that moment was thinking of nothing more exciting than obtaining a meal of some sort, for on reaching the street outside, he made straight towards a teashop on the opposite side of the road and entered through the swing doors.

'Well, that's that!' said Bobbie under his breath. 'I suppose I've got to hang about here while the beggar eats.'

He sauntered up the street and bought a paper to while away the time, never taking his eyes off the entrance to the teashop which sheltered his quarry. After about twenty minutes the man came out, and this time he was smoking a cigarette. Without hesitation, he re-crossed the road and once more entered the station and made for the Underground.

Hertford was too far behind to hear which station he booked to, for he dared not risk being spotted by the man, so he bought a ticket to the next station. Now came the difficulty. It was impossible for him to go down in the lift, which was evidently what the shadower intended doing, and if he went by the stairs he might lose him for good and all.

Well, it was the only way, anyhow, and Hertford decided to risk it. He took the stairs at a run and arrived at the bottom breathless, almost at the same time as the elevator. There was a train already in, and the man in the mackintosh made a dash for it. It was a south-bound train, and Hertford just managed to scramble into the next coach to his quarry as the gates closed. Bobbie kept his eyes glued to the window. Station after station passed, and the man made no move. At last they arrived at Clapham Common, and here the shadower alighted. Bobbie gave him time to reach the exit before he did likewise.

The man walked rapidly towards the lifts, and the secretary again took the risk and went up by the stairs. The lift arrived first this time, and Hertford was only just in time to see the back of his quarry as he turned out of the station and sharply to his right, along the south side of the

Common. For some two hundred yards he continued in this direction, and then struck off at an oblique angle across the Common towards the north side. Hertford had to keep well in the rear, for very little cover was afforded him here. But luckily the man in front seemed to have no suspicion that he was being tracked, for he kept steadily on, and only once turned his head to look back, when Hertford managed to slip behind a tree.

The road led round the north side and the man in the mackintosh followed it round, striding on down the street until he had nearly drawn level with Elmers Avenue. Here he crossed the road abruptly and entered a fair-sized house which stood facing the Common.

From the fact that he let himself in with a latchkey, Hertford deduced that this was the end of the chase, and that the mysterious shadower lived there. Walking on past the house, he noticed that the number was 48, and turned the corner down Elmers Avenue. Here he halted to think. What should be his next move?

Should he go back at once and report

to his employer, or should he hang about a bit and try and gain more information? The sight of a postman further down the street decided him, and he strolled down to meet him coming up.

'Can you tell me whereabouts Mr. Tom Helsby lives?' he enquired as the postman drew level with him.

The man paused, scratched his upper lip, and replied that he hadn't the faintest idea. This was not surprising, since it had been the first name that had flashed into Hertford's head.

'I think it was 48 North Side,' Hertford went on, 'but I'm not sure.'

The postman shook his head. 'It ain't there,' he answered. 'Doctor Manning lives there.'

He walked on and Hertford remained for some minutes lost in thought, a puzzled frown on his face. Who on earth was Dr. Manning?

8

Trapped

In the meanwhile, Eustace Barrington, having cleverly eluded his shadowers, hurried as quickly as possible back to his house in Welbeck Street, and here he discovered that a visitor awaited him in the form of a good-looking fresh-complexioned young man of between thirty and thirty-three. He introduced himself as Wallace Manton.

'I'm the junior partner in the firm of Manton, Topp and Manton,' he explained as he shook hands with the scientist. 'Of course I've heard a lot about you, Professor Barrington, but have never had the pleasure of meeting you before.'

Barrington led the way into his study. 'In what way can I be of assistance?' he asked as he pushed forward a chair for his visitor.

'Well,' began Manton, refusing the

cigar which Barrington offered him, 'my firm has for some time acted in the interests of the late James Lessard, and some three years ago our client left in our charge a sealed envelope, with instructions that it was to be opened immediately after his death.

'Of course, directly we received the news of his tragic end, we complied with his instructions and opened the envelope. Inside was another, also sealed, and addressed to 'Moira Lessard — my wife — to be delivered to her immediately after my decease,' followed by an address in Liverpool. You can imagine our astonishment, Professor Barrington, for we had not the least idea that Lessard was married. We at once communicated with the address in Liverpool, but while we were waiting for a reply, I heard from Detective Inspector Evens that the lady is now in London. He gave me her address and I called to see her, and she it was who suggested that the letter should be opened in your presence. She said if I would come on here, she would follow immediately.'

'Did you leave the letter with her?'

asked Barrington.

'I offered to, but she wouldn't take it. She said she would do nothing without your advice.' At that moment, Mrs. Timpson tapped at the door and announced that a lady wanted to see the scientist.

'Ask her to step up,' said Barrington as he turned to Wallace Manton. 'I expect that's Mrs. Lessard now.'

A moment later, the woman entered the room. Although still pale, she looked much better for her night's rest, and as Wallace Manton gazed at her, he thought he had seldom seen such a picture of entrancing loveliness.

Barrington bowed and wheeled forward a chair, into which she sank, her little gloved hands clasped in her lap.

'I wouldn't take the letter, Professor Barrington,' she said, smiling slightly at the scientist. 'I felt sure that you'd be interested to hear its contents, and I'd much prefer that it should be opened in your presence.'

Barrington thanked her, and the young lawyer took a long, sealed envelope from his breast pocket and handed it to her.

'There you are, Mrs. Lessard,' he said. 'I have now carried out my instructions, and will wish you both good day.' He picked up his hat and stick. 'If at some future time I can be of any further assistance to you, I shall only be too happy.'

'Thank you,' she said gratefully, 'but if you could spare the time, I should like you also to hear the contents of this letter.'

The young man laid down his hat and stick with alacrity. 'I must own that I'm very curious,' he said, smiling.

'Then,' said Professor Barrington, 'we won't put your curiosity to too great a strain. With Mrs. Lessard's permission, we'll open the letter at once.'

She handed it to him without a word, and the scientist broke the seal. The envelope contained a single sheet of foolscap paper and another smaller envelope.

'Please read it, Professor,' said Moira quietly.

Barrington laid the smaller envelope on the table and paused for a second, turning the paper over and over in his firm fingers. Then, in his deep well-modulated voice, he began.

107

"You will not receive this until either from natural causes, or possibly another reason, I shall have ceased to exist.

"The same hand which I feel sure was accountable for your father's mysterious disappearance is outstretched also over me, and daily, nay, hourly, I am expecting it to fall and crush me.

"Of the secret which existed between your father and myself I cannot speak, for I feel that already I have brought sufficient trouble upon you, and to reveal that secret to you would be but to expose you to the same danger that threatens me now. Beside which, without your father — and there seems little hope of ever seeing him now — the secret is lost forever.

"Enclosed in the same envelope as this letter is my will, duly signed and witnessed. I have left all my property, such as it is, both real and personal, to you, unconditionally. I feel that this is as your father would have wished. Had things turned out differently, you would have been a rich woman, but perhaps it is for the best that fate has willed otherwise.

" 'It was wrong of me to have ever allowed your father to persuade me to consent to our marriage, but by the time this letter reaches you, that wrong, at least, will have been righted.

" 'JAMES LESSARD'.'

For some seconds after the professor finished reading, there was silence. Then Barrington picked up the smaller envelope.

'This, I presume, contains the will,' he remarked as he slipped his forefinger under the flap and broke the seal. It proved to be a very brief document, merely, in a few words, bequeathing everything 'to my wife, Moira Lessard'.

'I wonder why he kept it such a secret, even from us, his lawyers,' said Manton. 'I never knew he'd even made a will. In fact, I'd often mentioned it, but he always made some evasive reply and changed the subject. I'm afraid, Mrs. Lessard,' he continued with a smile, 'your inheritance is not a large one. Of course, we haven't been fully into the matter yet, but I think it amounts to considerably under £2,000.'

She smiled faintly. 'I'm not thinking so

much about the money,' she answered. 'I was hoping that the letter would throw some light upon my father's disappearance and mysterious death. Oh, Mr. Barrington — ' She turned her large violet eyes on the scientist. ' — what do you think can be the meaning of it all? What was this danger that appears to have threatened both my father and Mr. Lessard?'

Eustace Barrington shook his head.

'I don't know, Mrs. Lessard,' he admitted, 'but I mean to find out. It was undoubtedly, as events have proved, no mere shadowy illusion, but a very real and tangible fact. One thing strikes me about Lessard's letter. In his concluding sentence, he says 'that wrong, at least, will have been righted.' The 'at least' suggests that there were other wrongs which had not, and could not, be righted.'

The young lawyer looked up interestedly. 'You mean, Professor, that probably Lessard had done someone wrong, and that it was this person or persons from whom he feared some sort of retribution?'

'But what about my father?' interposed Moira. 'Mr. Lessard says in his letter that the same danger threatened my father. Surely no one would blame my father for something Mr. Lessard had done?'

Wallace Manton shot a quick glance at the professor. 'There's some truth in that,' he remarked.

Barrington smiled. 'You forget,' he said, quietly, 'that whatever it was, this danger that Lessard talks about was equally shared by your father, for it appears to be closely connected with the secret which was apparently known only to Mr. Brennan and James Lessard.'

'But,' said Mrs. Lessard, 'what can this terrible secret be? The greatest mystery to me is where my father can have been during the time he disappeared and the time he reappeared again so mysteriously at Copthorn House. I'm sure he would not have gone away willingly without leaving me some word. He would never have caused me all that terrible anxiety of his own free will. And then his dreadful death. Who could have been the man who shot him?' Tears sprang to her eyes as she thought of it. 'If we'd only known he was there, we might have saved him.'

Eustace Barrington crossed over to her side and laid his hand gently on her shoulder. 'My dear Mrs. Lessard,' he said kindly, 'you can rest assured that I'll leave no stone unturned to discover who was responsible for your father's death — that I shall not rest until I have brought the guilty person to justice. In the meantime, you must try and bear up, and be as patient as possible.'

Moira took a handkerchief from her bag and dabbed her eyes. 'I know that you'll do your best, Professor,' she said, gratefully as she rose to her feet. 'I don't know what I should have done, but for your kindness. It would have been dreadful to have been alone here in London without anyone to turn to, or to seek advice from.'

The young lawyer rose. 'I hope, Mrs. Lessard,' he said, 'that you'll also look upon me as a friend, and if there's anything I can do to assist you in any way, I shall be only too willing.'

She gave him a grateful look. 'It's very good of you,' she said sweetly. 'I think I'll be getting back to the hotel now. I have some shopping to do this afternoon.' She held out a small hand to the professor. 'Goodbye for the present, Mr. Barrington.'

'Goodbye, Mrs. Lessard,' said Barrington as he took her hand in his. 'By the way,' he added in a lower voice, 'are you all right for money? If not, please allow me to be your banker temporarily.'

'I have quite sufficient,' she answered, 'but it was awfully kind of you to think of it.'

Barrington stepped to the door and held it open. Wallace Manton picked up his hat and stick.

'If you'll allow me,' he said to Mrs. Lessard, 'I'll walk back with you as far as your hotel. Goodbye, Professor.'

Eustace Barrington smiled faintly to himself as they passed out. The young lawyer's interest in his late client's widow was obviously not entirely of a professional nature.

The woman, too, in spite of her trouble, seemed to welcome his escort. Well, they were both young, and possibly Manton would help to prevent her thinking too much about her father and brooding over his death.

The scientist selected a cigar, and having lighted it, sank into his comfortable armchair, and sat for some time thinking and blowing clouds of fragrant smoke ceiling-wards. Suddenly he rose to his feet and crossed to the bookcase which housed the famous index.

For years, Barrington, interested as he was in the study of humanity, had made a practice of compiling in this index all sorts of stray information, and there was scarcely an item of news of any description that was likely to prove of interest in his hobby of criminology, or was in any way connected with crime in all its aspects, that did not hold some sort of record in the index. Hertford made a practice of keeping it up to date for him, and found it a most congenial job.

For the best part of the afternoon Barrington delved among its pages, and darkness had fallen before he finally snapped shut the volume he had been searching through, and returned it to its place on the shelves. But his eyes with their piercing intentness would have told Hertford, had he been present, that his employer had lighted upon a fresh discovery, a discovery that had apparently filled him with elation.

One of the maids brought tea, and Barrington was in the act of sipping a cup of the steaming beverage when the telephone bell rang sharply. Setting his cup on the table, he crossed to the instrument.

'Hullo! Hullo!' said a gruff voice in his ear. 'Is that Professor Barrington?'

The scientist replied in the affirmative.

'This is Sergeant Wilson,' went on the voice. 'I'm speaking for Detective Inspector Evens. He wants you to meet him at once at 20 Margrave Street. It's just off the Kennington Road. He's made a sensational discovery in connection with the Lessard case, and he wants you to bring the tooth with you.'

'I'll be along directly,' answered Barrington, and he hung up the receiver. For some minutes after he stood motionless, his fingers twisting his ring, staring into space. Then he again picked up the telephone.

'That Scotland Yard?' he asked after he had given the number. There was a pause, then: 'I want to speak to Detective Inspector Evens. Oh, is that you, Carter? He's out, is he? This is Eustace Barrington speaking — is Sergeant Wilson there? Went out with Evens early this afternoon? All right — no, there's no message, thanks.' He rang off.

On the face of it, the message appeared to be genuine. Barrington hastily finished his tea, and having scribbled a note for Hertford and placed it on his desk, left the house. In Welbeck Street he hailed a taxi, instructing the driver to put him down at the end of Margrave Street.

What had Evens discovered? he wondered. And for what reason did he want the tooth? Could he have found out the meaning of the little steel ball? Most probably he had discovered the identity of the woman who had sent the first James Lessard the note begging him to meet her on the Embankment.

The more Barrington pondered over that side of the case, the more he became convinced that that crime had been an error on the part of the criminal, and that the man on the Albert Embankment had met his death solely because he happened to bear the same name as Lessard the explorer. There was no other possible reason to account for it.

In that case, the person or persons responsible for the murder of the owner of Copthorn House could not have known him personally — only by name — and equally certain that he must have been unknown by him. The hazy, indefinite theory which had built itself up in Barrington's brain was every moment becoming clearer, and his long search of the index had supplied him with what he was convinced was the missing link in the chain, namely, the motive behind the whole mysterious business.

The only point that baffled him was the disappearance of Moira Lessard's father and his subsequent reappearance at Copthorn House on the day that Lessard had been murdered. He was still pondering over this, lost in his own thoughts, when the taxi stopped and recalled him to himself.

Margrave Street proved to be a dark, narrow thoroughfare, dimly lighted, and the rickety houses that lined the street on either side were in the last stages of dilapidation, and appeared likely to fall down at any moment. Raucous-voiced children with wizened half-starved faces played in the roadway and shouted after Barrington as he passed. It was a typical slum. One of those streets that are half alleys, of which there are all too many on the outskirts of the great metropolis, and which breed vice and crime as a pestilential swamp breeds mosquitoes. Few of the houses contained a window that was not broken, and number twenty differed not at all in this respect from the rest. It was, if anything, dirtier and more ramshackle than the others, and Barrington surveyed for some seconds before he applied his hand to the rusty knocker and rapped loudly. Almost instantly there was the sound of a step in the passage, and the door was opened.

'Is that Professor Barrington?' enquired a voice — the same voice that had spoken to the detective over the telephone. "am Detective Sergeant Wilson. Inspector Evens is upstairs waiting for you. Will you go up?'

Barrington could dimly make out the

figure of a short burly man in the darkness as he stepped into the passage. Instantly the door closed behind him.

'If you will wait a minute, sir,' continued the gruff voice, 'I'll strike a match.'

Suddenly something — a sixth sense — seemed to warn Barrington of danger; but even as he turned sharply, something soft but heavy descended upon his head, a shattering red-hot pain seared his brain, and with a fiery curtain flecked with green flashes dancing before his eyes, his senses swam and he knew no more.

9

The Two Steel Balls

For what length of time he remained unconscious, Eustace Barrington had not the slightest idea. He regained his senses to find himself lying on a couch in a strange room, a lamp on a rickety table in the middle flooding the place with light. That was what attracted his attention first, because the light hurt his eyes and his head was throbbing violently, as though some one were beating time to a diabolical tattoo upon it.

He closed his eyes against the light. Where was he? What had happened? Ah! He remembered now. The message from Evens. Of course, it had been a trap. He moved first one leg, and then the other. His ankles had been securely bound. His hands also were bound behind his back. His fingers resting upon the couch supplied him with the information that it was upholstered in worn leather.

Barrington opened his eyes again and glanced curiously around him. The room was small and dirty, and from the walls the paper hung in strips, revealing the plaster beneath, while in several places the plaster itself had fallen, leaving the laths behind bare.

The floor was devoid of carpet, and the broken boards were as filthy as the rest of the apartment. In the middle of this uninviting room stood a plain, rickety deal table, one corner supported on an empty beer box on which was a smoking paraffin lamp. Two plain wooden chairs completed the entire furniture. On the opposite side of the room to Barrington was a small window, which at the moment was covered by heavy wooden shutters secured by an iron bar.

The professor lay perfectly still, and his brain, in spite of his throbbing aching head, was at work, keen and alert. The whole thing was plain, of course. He had been decoyed here in order that they could secure the contents of the tooth! The mysterious prowler at Copthorn House must have in some way discovered that Harrington had got it in his possession; had possibly been still lurking in the vicinity when the professor had discovered it. Hence the watcher outside the house in Welbeck Street.

And what had happened to Hertford? Had he, too, been caught? A spasm of uneasiness passed through Barrington as the thought entered his mind. He would never forgive himself if anything had happened to Bobbie. If Barrington's theory were correct, these people — for he was now assured that there were more than one — were playing for enormous stakes, and would stick at nothing to achieve their ends. They had already given ample proof of that.

He tried to moisten his lips, but the movement gave him a twinge of pain, and for the first time he became aware that a gag had been thrust between his teeth. A feeling of impotence swept over him as he realised how easily he had fallen into the trap so neatly set for him. Had they already taken the tooth from where it had reposed in his waistcoat pocket? It was impossible to find out, but he concluded that they had.

Barrington began to try and see if there was any chance of wriggling free of the bonds that held him, but in spite of his repeated efforts they refused to give an inch, and the exertion only added to the violent throbbing of his head, so that in the end he was compelled to desist. Panting for breath, he lay still at ease, the perspiration standing out on his forehead.

Suddenly a sharp sound from outside the room reached his ears: a creak of a loose floorboard. Someone was coming along the passage. In an instant, Barrington relaxed his muscles so that his limbs went limp and lifeless. It was to his advantage to pretend to remain unconscious.

The handle of the door clicked, and the next moment a man stepped softly into the room. From beneath half-closed lids, the scientist surveyed the newcomer. He was a tall man, dressed in a dark overcoat, the collar of which was turned up about his ears. He wore a soft hat, the brim pulled low over his eyes, but his face was concealed beneath a silk handkerchief of some dark material which covered his chin, mouth and nose, and only left his eyes visible.

He paused inside the doorway for a second, and stood looking at the professor. Then he crossed over to the couch and looked closely into Barrington's face. Barrington completely closed his eyes, and lay still as a log. He could feel the other's breath as it fanned his cheek. All at once the man stretched out his hand and suddenly raised the scientist's right eyelid, but, with quick presence of mind, he had just time to roll his eyes upwards so that only the whites were visible. Apparently satisfied, the man in the mask left the couch and walked over to the table.

Barrington gave a little motionless sigh of relief. The ordeal had been a great strain, even to his trained steel-like nerves.

After a moment, he ventured once more to open his eyes the fraction of an inch. The man was examining something in the light of the lamp. A little thrill shot through the professor's body as he saw that it was the tiny steel ball he had found in Lessard's tooth. After a little while, the masked man laid it down on the table and fumbled in his pocket, and produced a small pill-box. Removing the lid, he tipped the contents out into the palm of his left hand, and putting the box on the table, picked the steel ball up again, placing it beside the other object in his hand. A little murmur of satisfaction escaped him.

Barrington opened his eyes wide for a second. As the man held his hand under the light, the scientist could plainly see the contents. There were now two steel balls precisely alike in appearance and size.

Barrington shut his eyes again. Where had the second ball come from? Ah! Of course — he remembered the missing tooth from Brennan's mouth. The other ball had been contained in that, and the mysterious individual in the mask had got it. Then at some time shortly before his death, old Brennan must have been in his power. Perhaps that was where he had been since his disappearance.

In that case, why had there been a

delay of nearly three years before any attempt had been made to secure the second tooth from Lessard? Also, the tooth had only recently been extracted from Brennan's mouth, certainly not more than three days before his death. If he had been in the hands of the masked man ever since his disappearance, why had he made no effort to secure the tooth previously?

Barrington's thoughts were switched suddenly back to the present by the sound of a second step outside, and another man entered the room. It was the man who had been watching in Welbeck Street that morning.

'Well, Doctor,' he said as he advanced to the table, where the masked man was still examining the little objects in his palm.

'Everything is exceedingly well, my friend,' answered the man addressed as Doctor, in a curious grating voice, with the hint of a hiss in it which reminded Barrington of a venomous reptile. 'After nearly three years I've managed to lay my hands on these at last.' There was a note of triumph in his voice as he pointed to the contents in his left hand.

The other man looked at the little balls wit, an expression of curiosity on his wolfish face. 'What are they?' he asked.

'They represent a fortune,' replied the Doctor with a little sibilant chuckle as he transferred them back to the pill-box and placed it carefully back in his inside pocket. His companion grunted.

'I don't see why you should be so blooming close about it,' he grumbled. 'You never would tell me what it was all about. Why can't you tell me the meaning of it all?'

The masked man turned on his confederate with a snarl.

'Do you think I'm a fool?' he grated. 'If I let you know as much as I know, I should probably end up with a knife in my back while you walked off with the lot, instead of the share you've been promised. It's enough for you to know that in less than three days from now, you'll be a rich man.'

'I suppose I've got to take your word for it,' said the other man dubiously. 'At least you might tell me one thing. Where's this bloomin' fortune to be found?'

The doctor eyed him for a moment in silence.

'You want to know a lot, don't you,' he remarked at length. 'Well, I don't know that it matters very much if you do know.' He chuckled below his breath. 'It's in the Safe Deposit Company's vaults in Victoria Street.'

The man stared at him in astonishment. 'But surely — ' he began, when the other cut him short.

'I'm not going to stop here all night answering questions,' he snarled. 'Get that straw, and look sharp about it!'

Grumbling, the other man left the room, and Barrington, his brain working at express speed, rapidly thought over this fresh information. Was the man called Doctor serious when he mentioned the Safe Deposit, or had he been pulling the other man's leg? And what on earth did he want the straw for?

Suddenly a ghastly explanation flashed through Barrington's brain. They were going to set fire to the place! His premonition was confirmed when the other man returned, his arms filled with bundles of straw which he dumped down in the middle of the floor. The man in the mask produced a short end of candle from his pocket, and having lighted it, extinguished the oil lamp.

With his handkerchief he removed the hot chimney, and setting it on the table, proceeded to thoroughly soak the straw and surrounding floor with oil from the lamp.

Having done so, he flung the lamp into a corner, and shot a keen glance round the room.

'Go on,' he said to the other man, who had stood watching him. 'There's nothing more to remain here for. I don't think Professor Barrington will bother me anymore.'

With a last look round, he picked up the end of the candle and carefully set it in the middle of the straw! Then, swiftly gliding to the door, he passed out with his companion.

The perspiration broke out clammily on Eustace Barrington's forehead as he realised the devilish ingenuity of the plan. The end of the candle could, at the most, only last for another ten minutes, and then it would reach the oil-soaked straw, and in less than three minutes the room would be a raging furnace! And he was a prisoner bound and helpless!

He had often found himself in a tight corner through his interest in criminology, but never such a hopeless one as this.

Vainly he strove to loosen the cords which bound him, but they had been tied by a skilful hand, and he only succeeded in cutting the flesh about his wrists. He worked his jaw about, to try and loosen the gag from between his teeth, but to no purpose. By a prodigious effort of will, he regained his calm, and rapidly his brain worked in an effort to evolve a means of escape.

Somewhere outside, a church clock chimed eight, and in the silence of the room he could hear the shrill laughter of the children playing in the streets below. If he could only attract somebody's attention! But gagged as he was, it was impossible.

Slowly the candle burnt steadily on. Not more than an inch separating it from the straw! He thought of trying to roll himself off the couch and across the floor to the candle, but dismissed the idea almost before it had been formed. The candle was so precariously balanced amongst the straw that the slightest touch might overturn it and precipitate the catastrophe.

He was helpless. This must be the end. A wave of fury against the inhuman monster who had planned such a diabolical death surged over the scientist. To die like a rat in a trap, without being able to make any attempt to save himself . . .

His thoughts turned to Hertford. He hoped nothing had happened to him. Heaven help him if he, too, had fallen into the clutches of this fiendish scoundrel. He twisted onto his face, and as he did so, his automatic petrol lighter, which he kept in an upper pocket of his waistcoat, dropped out onto the couch. It must have been only partly put back after the masked man had searched him for the contents of the second tooth. Here was a gleam of hope! If he could only succeed in getting it into his fingers and press the catch, it would ignite by the mere fact of opening, and he could burn the cords which bound his wrists.

Barrington turned over again onto his back, and inch by inch edged his body up towards the head of the couch. At last, after what seemed an eternity, he felt the touch of the metal case against his wrists. Another inch, and he had grasped it between his fingers!

His wrists were raw where the cords cut into the flesh, and every movement sent an agony of pain through him; but he gritted his teeth, grasping the case as firmly as he could, and started to twist over again on to his face.

He glanced at the candle. Less than half an inch remained!

With infinite care, he felt for the catch and pressed it. The lid of the little lighter flew open, and as it did so, the force of the spring jerked it out of the professor's hand, and it fell with a clatter to the floor.

The last hope was gone!

10

Just in Time

After Hertford had made his discovery relating to the identity of the man who lived at 48 North Side, he was in somewhat of a quandary what to do next. Should he return forthwith to Welbeck Street and inform the professor of the result of his investigations, or should he make his way to the nearest telephone and acquaint him of the new facts in that way? Hertford paced thoughtfully up and down, thinking this out.

To both these proposals, the same difficulty presented itself. In either case, he would have to lose sight of the house containing the mysterious Dr. Manning and the man he himself had followed there.

It seemed to Bobbie that his time would be better employed watching the house, and trying to make some fresh discovery, than to leave it for however short a period while he went in search of a telephone. During his absence quite a lot might happen, and Hertford was too keen to risk the chance of missing anything, however trivial, that would be likely in any way to assist the professor in solving the problem in which he was engaged.

Having made up his mind, Bobbie at once proceeded to look for a convenient spot from where he would be able to keep the house under observation.

Forty-eight, like the other houses along North Side, faced the Common, and about a hundred yards to the right and nearly opposite the gate was a small clump of trees, by one of which Hertford espied a seat. The trees were old veterans, and their trunks consequently fairly large, sufficiently so at any rate to prevent anyone seated on the seat from being seen from the house. Hertford decided to take up his position on the seat, and crossing the road, slipped under the railing which bordered the Common from the pavement, and made his way to the clump of trees and the seat.

By sitting in one corner and screwing his body half round in a particularly uncomfortable position, he was able to keep his eyes fixed on the gate of 48. The day was a cold one, and a keen wind blew from across the Common, so that in a very little while Bobbie began to feel like a block of ice. He had eaten nothing since breakfast, and was starting to feel hungry.

An hour went slowly by, and he was beginning to get most decidedly fed up. He had been full of hope when he had started out, but the cold, combined with the feeling of emptiness in his inside, made him feel very sorry for himself, and come to the conclusion that life was, at the moment at any rate, hardly worth living.

Disgust was too mild a word to describe his feelings, as he reflected that at that moment most of the people in the houses around him were in the act of sitting down to a hearty lunch. Visions of roast lamb and beef floated before his eyes, and then he laughed.

'Well,' he said, stamping his feet to try

and restore feeling to his frozen toes, 'I'm not obliged to do this unless I care to do so. I was engaged as a secretary. Still, I'm glad it isn't all germs and bugs. This hobby of the professor's wakes things up a bit.'

Two more hours dragged slowly by, and they seemed to be the longest that Bobbie had ever experienced in his life. The red disc of the sun was sinking behind a cloud, and with the shadow of approaching darkness, a thin damp mist began to creep over the Common. The moisture penetrated beneath his overcoat and sent a shiver through him. Somewhere down the road the jingle of a bell came to his ears, and presently through the gathering gloom, he made out the figure of a muffin-man, his wares on a tray balanced on his head, doing his rounds. Bobbie eyed the tray longingly. He would have given anything at that moment for a plate of those muffins, piping hot, and a cup of steaming tea!

The sound of the bell grew fainter and fainter, and Hertford, drawing his coat closer around him, and trying to forget his hunger, continued his vigil.

Half an hour passed, and suddenly he sat up sharply, his senses keen and alert. The door of 48 had opened, and a stream of light poured down the path to the gate. Silhouetted against the light appeared the figures of two men. Hertford rose to his feet, stretching his cramped limbs with a sigh of relief. Something was moving at last!

Moving out at the gate, the two men turned sharply to the left and set off at a brisk pace up North Side, Hertford following in their wake. As they passed a street lamp, he could see that the shorter of the two was the man he had tracked earlier in the day. Presently they arrived at the Underground station, and here they paused for a moment and then crossed the road, heading for the post office, which they both entered.

Hertford strolled slowly past, and glanced through the window. The shorter man was in the act of looking through the pages of a telephone directory, and in a few seconds entered a public call box.

I wonder who he's ringing up, Bobbie

thought, little guessing that the call was to Eustace Barrington, and that the result was to place his employer in the direst peril he had ever experienced in his life!

In a few minutes, the men left the post office and made their way at once to the cab rank which lay just opposite. The taller man, who was so wrapped up in a thick muffler that try as he would Hertford could not get so much as a glimpse of his face, stepped into a taxi, while the other man gave a short direction to the driver and then followed his companion. The driver cranked up the engine, and as it spluttered into life, climbed into the seat and, with grating of gears, drove off.

Scarcely had they started before Hertford was in another cab and following close on their heels. Down the Clapham High Street they went, and evidently they had instructed their driver to hurry, for the pace was hot. Dodging in and out of the traffic, the cabs raced on, pausing only when they were held up in a traffic block at Kennington Gate.

I wish I knew where the dickens we

were going to, thought Bobbie while they waited for the constable on point duty to give the signal to go on. *This is like a game of blind man's buff, with me as the blind man.*

At last the taxi in front jerked away again, and presently swung round to Kennington Road. When it arrived at Lambeth Baths, it stopped. Hertford tapped at the window of his cab and picked up the speaking tube.

'Drive straight on, and round the corner into Lambeth Road, and slow down,' he instructed the driver. The man nodded, and as the taxi swung round and slowed up, Hertford sprang out and thrust some money into the man's hand.

'Go on — don't stop,' said Hertford, and the cab, gathering speed again, went down the street. Hertford hurried back to Kennington Road, and was just in time to see his quarry turn into a street on the other side.

He crossed the road and strolled to the turning down which they had disappeared. They had stopped about halfway down the street and were entering one of the dilapidated houses, and a moment later Bobbie heard the faint sound of a closing door. Apparently they had reached the end of their journey. He glanced up at the name on the wall. It was Margrave Street. For a few moments he lounged about at the corner, and then walked slowly down the dark and evil-looking slum. As he passed the door which the two men had entered, he gave a swift look up, and noticed that the number was twenty.

'What do we do now?' mused Harrington's secretary as he continued his way to the end of the narrow street. 'I wonder if they're coming out again, or whether they're going to stop there.' He paused and looked about him.

Another street similar to the one down which he had come crossed it at right angles. For a few yards down each side of this intersecting road ran a high, crumbling, dirty brick wall before a further string of miserable houses began. Obviously the houses to Margrave Street possessed back yards.

An idea flashed into Hertford's brain. He was sick and tired of hanging about waiting, and was intensely curious to discover what had brought the two men he had followed to this unsavoury neighbourhood. If he could get round to the back of number twenty, he might be able to find out what was going on inside. The thrill of adventure surged through Bobbie's young blood and made him forget all about his hunger. He decided to risk it.

Taking a swift glance round to assure himself that he was unobserved, he reached for the top of the wall, and gripping it with his strong fingers, gave a quick spring and hoisted himself to the top, and the next instant had dropped lightly into the filthy yard on the other side. Thus it was that he failed to see Eustace Barrington, who at that precise moment was knocking for admission on the door of number twenty.

Hertford landed on a heap of evil-smelling rubbish without a sound, and looked about him. The last house in Margrave Street on this side was number twenty-eight, so the lad calculated that the fifth backyard would belong to number twenty. Noiselessly Hertford began to pick his way across the tiny yard. Wooden fences divided the yards from each other. They were quite low, and in many cases in such a bad state of dilapidation that there was room to crawl through where the palings were broken away.

He had successfully negotiated the second yard, and was in the act of crossing the third when he stopped suddenly, his heart in his mouth, and crouched down behind a pile of old broken boxes. The crazy back door had opened, and a faint glimmer of light from a flaring gas jet within faintly illumined the backyard. A man attired in a trousers and shirt appeared, and crossed directly to where Bobbie was hiding.

He held his breath. Had he been discovered — seen from some upper window?

The man stopped when he had almost reached the pile of broken boxes behind which he had crouched, and Hertford heard the rattle of metal. A little sigh of relief escaped him, and his tense muscles relaxed. The man had only been to deposit some rubbish in the dustbin, and now, whistling softly below his breath, he was returning to the house. He re-entered the back door, but instead of shutting it behind him, as Bobbie had hoped he left it open, and taking a kettle from where it was boiling on a dirty gas stove, poured out some water into a dirty tin basin, and calmly proceeded to set about the job of shaving himself in a cracked mirror which hung below the gas jet, whistling all the while.

Hertford muttered anathemas upon the man under his breath. He dared not move from his place of concealment and risk being seen by the man in the scullery. The light, though dim, was sufficient to illumine the small size of the yard, and in order to reach the dividing fence he would have to expose himself directly in its rays.

There was nothing to do but wait where he was. In the meanwhile, his quarry might leave number twenty without his being any the wiser. Hertford gritted his teeth with impatience as the man, after shaving, proceeded to wash himself. At last a woman's voice shouted from somewhere inside the house.

''Urry up, Jim,' she called. 'We shan't 'alf be late.'

The man growled something in reply, and kicked the door open. Hertford waited for several minutes before he moved, and then, as everything remained quiet, ventured from his hiding-place. Only one back yard now separated him from his objective, and in a few seconds he had crossed this and was standing outside the back of number twenty.

He looked up at the house. It was in total darkness. Cautiously he edged his way to the back door, and felt for the handle. He expected it to be locked, but as his fingers closed round it and softly turned the knob, the door gave beneath his pressure.

Hertford hesitated for a second, listening intently, his ears strained to catch the slightest sound, but from within the house all was silent as the grave. A clock in the neighbourhood chimed the hour, and Hertford counted the strokes — eight o'clock.

Noiselessly he opened the door, and the next instant had slipped inside. Holding his breath, he paused and listened again. Absolute silence reigned within. Had his quarry already gone? Bobbie drew from his pocket his electric torch and flashed its beams around him. He was in the scullery of the house, and two broken steps led up to a bare and empty kitchen. The whole place was exceedingly dirty, and appeared, as far as he could see, to be entirely free from furniture of any kind. The floor was full of rat holes and thick with a carpet of dust that had certainly not been disturbed for months except by the passage of rats, whose tiny footprints were visible everywhere.

Hertford crept up the steps into the kitchen. The loose, rotten boards creaked beneath his weight, and he extinguished his torch, his heart thumping madly. Still no sound reached him from the silence of the house, and after a few minutes he went on again. The kitchen door, or what remained of it, for the upper panels were broken away, stood ajar, and the lad saw, as he switched on his light again, that it opened against a flight of stairs which appeared to lead to the upper part of the house.

He stepped through the kitchen door and found himself in a passage which led to the front door. Sweeping his light on the floor in front of him, he saw that here the dust had been disturbed, for a trail of confused footprints led from the door to the foot of the stairs.

Hertford was feeling fairly certain by this time that the house was deserted and his quarry had left, but at the same time someone might still be lurking in the upper regions. So, before attempting to ascend the stairs, he switched off his torch. Then he started to mount the stairs. Very slowly, without a sound — testing each step before he threw his body weight from one leg to the other — he reached the top of the stairs at last, and stopped to listen.

Suddenly to his straining ears came the sound of a sharp clatter of something falling on the floor. Hertford drew his breath sharply. So there was someone still in the house! He crept a little further forward, and now he could see something which the head of the stairs had previously hidden. A thin pencil of light which streamed from beneath a closed door on his right.

Even as he looked, the light seemed to grow brighter, and to flicker strangely. To his ears came a curious, ominous crackling sound. Hertford suddenly sniffed the air, and to his nostrils came the acrid smell of smoke combined with another smell — the odour of paraffin oil. In an instant he flashed on his torch again, and for a second its beams played upon the door from which the light was streaming. A thin volume of smoke was curling from beneath. Then Bobbie understood. The place was on fire.

He ran to the door, and bending down, applied his eye to the keyhole. The interior of the room was brilliantly lit with a sheet of flame which seemed to be shooting up from the middle of the floor, and the bright glare revealed to his astonished gaze the bound figure of a man on a couch directly opposite the

147

door. A volume of black acrid smoke blotted the scene out, but Bobbie had seen enough.

With a swift turn of the wrist he flung the door open, and guarding his face in the crook of his arm, rushed across to the couch. A cry escaped his lips as he recognised the figure on it.

'Good heavens!' he gasped. 'The professor!'

The fire was spreading rapidly, and already half the room was a blazing furnace as Hertford hurriedly untied the cords which bound the scientist's wrists and ankles, and removed the gag from between his teeth.

He had to half carry Eustace Barrington from the room, for the tight cords had stopped the circulation, and his limbs were for the moment numb and powerless. It was not until they were outside in the street that the professor spoke.

'Thanks, Bobbie!' was all he said, but there was a world of meaning in the pressure of his hand as it clasped Hertford's in a firm grip.

11

At the Safe Deposit

In a lofty and rather bleak-looking room, through the high curtainless windows of which could be obtained an excellent view of the Thames Embankment, had anyone wished to avail themselves of the opportunity, four people were seated on the morning following the events related in the previous chapter. It was early, for the time was scarcely nine. They consisted of Eustace Barrington, Bobbie Hertford, Detective-Sergeant Wilson, and Detective Inspector Evens.

The room was Evens' private room at Scotland Yard, and the worthy inspector was seated at his writing table, his elbows resting on the blotting pad, gently chewing a penholder.

Professor Barrington looked pale and slightly haggard, but otherwise seemed none the worse for his terrible experience of the night before. Although on leaving number twenty Barrington had immediately given the alarm, the house in Margrave Street had, in spite of the valiant efforts of the fire brigade, been completely gutted, and the firemen had all their work cut out to prevent the flames from spreading to the surrounding ramshackle old buildings in the street. After giving the alarm, Barrington and Hertford had returned to Welbeck Street, and the scientist had at once got on the phone to Inspector Evens, and briefly communicated to that worthy a short resumé of what had taken place.

Evens had wished to go immediately to the house on North Side, Clapham Common, and arrest the inmates, but Barrington had protested against this action, although he agreed with the inspector's suggestion that a plain-clothes man should be put on to watch the place. Having made an appointment to see Evens at Scotland Yard in the morning, he had retired to bed to snatch a night's much-needed rest.

'I'm blowed if I can see why we can't

arrest the beggars at once,' growled Evens as he paused for a moment in his occupation of chewing his penholder.

The professor smiled a trifle wearily. 'Because, my dear Evens,' he answered, 'you haven't an atom of evidence that's good enough to lay before a jury. A clever counsel would smash our case to pieces in no time. There's nothing to connect this Doctor Manning and his confederate with either of the murders, beyond the fact that he seemed anxious to obtain possession of the little steel ball which I found in Lessard's tooth. Certainly he was already in possession of the other steel ball, which I surmise came from the other tooth extracted from Brennan; but as far as a jury is concerned, we have no definite proof that there was anything concealed in Brennan's tooth.

'Of course we could arrest them for attempted murder in my case, but in that event we should probably lose all chance of solving the main problem. On the other hand, we've now got them at a disadvantage. In all probability they're feeling convinced that I've perished as they intended I should in the fire at Margrave Street, and will make the next move, feeling perfectly secure that the only person who might have stood in their way, who in any case could have discovered a clue to the meaning of the steel balls, was removed.'

'What do you think the next move will be then?' asked the inspector.

'The next move,' said Eustace Barrington quietly, 'unless I'm greatly mistaken, will take place at the Safe Deposit Company's premises in Victoria Street.'

Evens laughed. 'Do you mean you think they're going to burgle the place, Professor?' he demanded. 'Because if so, I — '

'Nothing so crude,' interposed the scientist, shaking his head.

'Then what on earth do you mean?' said Evens gruffly. 'It seems to me that you know a great deal more about this affair than you say. I've thought that all along. Why be so close about it?'

Barrington smiled at the worthy inspector's outburst. 'Because,' he answered, 'although I have a faint suspicion of the meaning of it all, I'm by no means sure. When I *am* sure, I'll tell you all about it;

but until then, Evens, you know me well enough by now to know that I must work in my own way.'

Inspector Evens cooled down somewhat. 'Oh, well, Professor,' he conceded grudgingly, 'I suppose there's always method in your madness, anyhow, I will say that.'

'Thanks, Evens,' said the scientist, with a twinkle in his dark eyes. 'Now,' he continued, 'you said on the telephone last night that you'd discovered the identity of the woman who wrote the note to Lessard asking him to meet her on the Embankment.'

Detective Inspector Evens turned to Sergeant Wilson. 'You tell Professor Barrington,' he ordered, 'exactly what you told me.'

Sergeant Wilson, a thin fair-haired man who possessed a remarkably high and somewhat squeaky voice, produced a notebook from his pocket, in all respects the twin brother of the one that Evens possessed. After consulting this for a moment, he began:

'According to instructions received

from Detective Inspector Evens,' he piped, 'I traced the messenger who had delivered the note to the porter at James Lessard's club. It was not a difficult task, and I found that the message had been handed in to one of the District Messenger offices at Charing Cross. Making enquiries of the messenger, I discovered that he remembered the letter very well. It had been handed in by a woman named Winifred Lawrence, who was a dancer in a Cabaret show at the Hotel Splendid, round the corner.

'The manager knew her quite well. From the management of the hotel, I obtained her address; she lives with her mother in a block of mansion flats which lie at the back of the Albert Embankment, between Westminster and Lambert Bridge, facing St. Thomas's Hospital. I called and interviewed her.

'It appears that James Lessard was an old friend of hers, and had known both herself and her mother for some years. She was very distressed when she learned of his mysterious death. As she had not seen a paper, I was the first to acquaint her of the fact. She admitted sending the note, and after some persuasion informed me of the reason. Her mother, it appears, had been ailing for some time with an infection of the lungs, and the doctors had at last informed her that unless she could send her mother abroad to a warmer climate, there was no chance of her living through the winter.

'She was very worried because she hadn't the money to send her mother away, and then an idea occurred to her that perhaps Mr. Lessard would lend her the amount. As she had no time to see him before, she made the appointment for after her show at the hotel, which finishes at a quarter to twelve.

'She made the meeting-place on the Albert Embankment because she didn't want her mother to know what she was going to ask Mr. Lessard for, as it would have only worried her, and her mother would probably not have allowed her to do it.' Sergeant Wilson paused, and turned over a leaf of his book before proceeding.

'It appears she never kept that appointment. Mr. Lessard, she says, rang up the hotel about nine to say that he couldn't keep the appointment that night, but would call and see her in the morning. She didn't take the message herself, but it was written down and brought to her dressing-room.'

Sergeant Wilson closed his book with a snap as he finished.

'So you see, Professor,' said Inspector Evens, 'that the thread has snapped. Whoever it was who rang Miss Lawrence up at the hotel, it could not have been Lessard, for at that time he was at Bolton's flat, and Bolton swears that he never used the telephone.'

Barrington looked thoughtfully out of the window.

'Whoever it was,' he remarked at length, 'they must have known in some way the contents of the note. Who was with Lessard when he received it at the club?'

'I made particular enquiries with regard to that point, sir,' said Sergeant Wilson again consulting his notebook. 'The page who handed him the letter says that Mr. Lessard was talking to Mr. Bolton, and to a Mr. De Castro who was not a member of the club but had been there two or three times with Mr. Lessard. I tried to find Mr. De Castro, to question him; his address was in a letter found in Lessard's pocket, but I discovered that he'd left the hotel at which he was staying that same evening, and the management had no idea where he had gone.'

A little gleam shot into the professor's eyes, but they were half closed, and it was unnoticed by the others. Every fresh fact seemed to strengthen and confirm his theory. His next remark caused Inspector Evens and Hertford to stare at him in astonishment.

'I wonder, Evens,' he said, 'if you would look me up a record of Amos Keller.'

Inspector Evens ran his finger despairingly through his bristly hair.

'Amos Keller?' he repeated stupidly.

Barrington nodded slowly.

'Commonly called Radiant Keller, I believe,' he said, 'from his habit of never touching anything but diamonds, and the — '

'I know who you mean,' broke in Evens. 'The man who was suspected of getting away with the famous Vandevere collection of diamonds about five years ago. The collection included the Vandevere Star, supposed to be the second largest diamond in the world. The thief broke into the strongroom at Vandevere Hall and got away with the lot. The whole affair bore the stamp of being Keller's work, but we couldn't bring it home to him. He died somewhere abroad a few years ago.'

'I know,' murmured Eustace Barrington, 'but all the same, I should like the records if you could let me have them.'

'What in the world has Amos Keller, who's been dead for years, got to do with the present case?' roared the exasperated inspector.

'If Radiant Keller hadn't died a few years ago,' said the professor slowly, 'there would not have been any present case.'

Evens gave a gesture of despair. 'If you will talk in riddles, I give it up,' he grumbled. 'But honestly, Professor, I don't in the least know what you're driving at. Do you really want Keller's record?'

'Most certainly I do,' replied the scientist. 'I should be glad if you could have it sent round to Welbeck Street this afternoon.' He glanced at his watch. 'I must be going now, Evens,' he continued. 'I'll let you know directly anything happens.'

He gripped the burly Inspector's hand. There was a genuine friendship between the Scotland Yard man and the eminent scientist, and if Evens did occasionally get a trifle exasperated at Barrington's manner, he recalled gratefully the number of times he had given him help. He knew well enough that Barrington could be relied upon to lay his cards down on the table at the proper moment, and until that time arrived, the only thing to do was to wait as patiently as possible.

What was at the back of the scientist's mind, Evens hadn't the slightest idea, but of one thing he was certain. Whatever it was, it boded ill for the mysterious and sinister Dr. Manning and his equally mysterious associate. Once Barrington got interested in a case, he never left it until it was solved, and as the scientist and his secretary left the room, Evens smiled to himself as he once more sat down to his desk, for he knew it was only a question of time before the fate of Dr. Manning was sealed.

As Barrington and Bobbie passed under the arch leading from Scotland Yard into Whitehall, Big Ben chimed the three-quarters after nine. The scientist struck across the road, and a few minutes later was striding down Victoria Street. He was very thoughtful and preoccupied, and Hertford, who knew his employer well in this mood, tactfully refrained from asking questions. At the same time he was bursting with curiosity, and it required a strong effort of will on his part to keep silent.

He guessed that the destination of their present excursion was the Safe Deposit Company's offices, and in this he proved correct, though for what reason they were going there he hadn't the faintest idea.

Barrington gave a quick glance to right and left as they arrived at the door of the building, and then, entering, he walked up to the counter, and giving his card to a clerk, asked to see the manager. Gazing in some awe at the famous name on the card, the clerk hurried off. He was gone some time before he returned and requested Professor Barrington to follow him. To Hertford's disappointment, the scientist asked him to wait, and followed the clerk.

It was nearly half an hour before Barrington returned, but there was a smile of satisfaction on his mobile features when he did so. He still remained silent, however, as they left the building and retraced their steps up Victoria Street. At last Hertford could contain himself no longer.

'Won't you tell me, sir,' he burst out curiously, 'why you called in there?'

The professor looked up abstractedly. 'Because, my boy,' he replied, 'in there lies the heart of the mystery.' And he relapsed into silence.

12

Escape!

On the way back to Welbeck Street, the professor remained lost in his own thoughts, while Hertford was so thoroughly bewildered that try as he would, and rack his brains as he might, he could not straighten out a single coherent theory from the mass of thoughts which seethed about in his brain.

One after another, questions poured through his mind. Who was Doctor Manning, and what connection was there between the dead jewel thief and the present case? Was it possible that he and the man known as Doctor Manning were one and the same, and that Keller was not dead after all? Then there was this visit to the Safe Deposit. What was the meaning of that? Barrington had said that the heart of the mystery lay there. But what was the heart of the mystery? As far as Bobbie could make out, there was neither a heart nor anything else to the mystery. It was just a senseless jumble, without rhyme or reason.

He had reached this stage when Barrington stopped at a telegraph office and despatched a long cablegram. As he handed it in, Hertford caught sight of the address. It was to a man who acted as agent for the scientist in Cairo! More mystery. Hertford gave it up in the end, and walked alongside Barrington, letting his thoughts wander where they would.

They arrived at Welbeck Street at last, and Eustace Barrington made at once for his study, where, without more ado, he recommenced his pacing up and down as though the peril of the burning house had never been; and as he paced he twisted his ring rhythmically from right to left.

On these occasions, Barrington was about as communicative as the proverbial oyster, and Hertford, after trying vainly to draw his employer into conversation and receiving only monosyllabic replies, contented himself by securing the index and pasting therein the cuttings which had accumulated on his desk during the past few days. It was the secretary's habit to scan all the morning and evening papers and to clip out any particular paragraph that had any bearing on criminology, or was likely to be useful for future information. On more than one occasion, the items of news thus obtained had proved of incalculable value to Barrington during the investigation of a case. Having exhausted the store of clippings on his desk, Hertford turned his attention to that morning's papers. He had not gone very far in his perusal of them before he came across an account of the fire at Margrave Street. It was the usual description of such a catastrophe, but a short paragraph at the end arrested the secretary's attention.

'Amongst the smouldering debris,' he read, 'has been discovered what appears to be the charred remains of a body. Inquiries are being made, but at present it is impossible to state whether the remains are those of a human being or an animal.'

Hertford smiled to himself. In this he recognised the hand of Eustace Barrington. The scientist had evidently taken steps to make certain that when Dr. Manning and his confederate read the account of the fire, they should receive confirmation of the fact that Barrington had perished in the holocaust. Throughout the morning, the secretary continued his work, and Barrington still sat silent, only moving from his chair when Mrs. Timpson appeared to announce that lunch was served.

The professor ate little, but Hertford found that excitement was as good as an aperitif and consumed enough for at least two, blaming his appetite on his long walk that morning in the cold sharp air, which he said had made him ravenously hungry. The meal was barely finished when a messenger arrived with a bulky packet for Professor Barrington. It was from Detective Inspector Evens, and contained the record of Amos Keller, for which Barrington had asked. The scientist carried it off to his study and settled down to a perusal of its pages, now and again making a brief note on a pad which he balanced on the arm of his chair. Hertford, having completed his work on the index, looked in the professor's book of engagements. There were a series of lectures ahead on 'Cosmic Forces', which would need some preparation, and he busied himself at the well-stocked bookshelves, gathering together such volumes as might be needed for reference. He had a feeling that it would not be long now before the professor would have finished with the present case, and life would resume its usual routine until another case arose which presented unusual features. Yet he himself could see no way out of the labyrinth.

What was the meaning of this period of seeming inactivity? Surely it was possible to be doing something? What was likely to happen next, and when would the riddle be solved? He glanced over at the professor. The scientist had finished his investigation of the records of Radiant Keller, and was lying back in his chair with half-closed eyes, the ceaseless twisting of the ring on his finger being the only sign that he was awake.

The warmth of the room and the silence at last had the effect of making Hertford feel drowsy, and he closed his eyes and dropped into a doze.

He awoke sharply, the insistent buzzing of the telephone ringing in his ears. Barrington had already sprung into activity, and in two strides had reached the instrument.

'Hello — yes — Eustace Barrington speaking,' he said into the receiver. 'Good! Make any excuse to keep him there — I'll be right along.' The scientist banged the receiver back on its hook and threw back his head. 'Get your coat on, Hertford,' he said, 'and come along with me.'

He hurried to the hall as he spoke for his own coat and hat, and a few minutes later, with Hertford by his side, he was out in Welbeck Street and hailing a passing taxi.

'Safe Deposit, Victoria Street,' he said to the driver as he sprang into the vehicle. 'And don't stop for anything.'

Barrington, his eyes gleaming with excitement, sat back in the cab as the driver let in his clutch with a bang and sent the car spinning along Welbeck Street at top speed. The scientist's face was tense and rigid, and he looked straight before him, his mind apparently fixed upon some approaching crisis. Hertford guessed that they were nearing the climax of the problem, though what was going to take place he hadn't the remotest idea.

In an almost incredibly short space of time, for the driver had broken all speed limits, and more than once had only slowed down in the nick of time to prevent being caught by a watchful policeman, they swung into Victoria Street, and a second later drew up outside the Safe Deposit. Eustace Barrington hardly waited for the taxi to stop before he sprang out, telling the driver to wait, and hurried into the building, followed by his secretary. The manager, a stout bald-headed little man with the tiniest moustache Bobbie had ever seen, was waiting for them just outside. He was obviously exceedingly nervous and uncomfortable, for he hurried forward to meet Barrington as he caught sight of the scientist's well-cut figure with an expression of the most profound relief on his chubby face.

'Thank heaven you've arrived, Professor,' was his greeting. 'He's downstairs in the vaults now. I kept him talking as long as I possibly could without arousing his suspicions, but he seemed in the deuce of a hurry, and at last I had to take him down.'

Professor Barrington wasted not a moment in words. 'You wait here, Hertford,' he directed. 'I'll go down below to the vaults with Mr. Atherstone.' He indicated the manager. 'Keep your eyes open, Bobbie, and if there should be any trouble, stop anyone from leaving the building. You'd better take this.' He slipped something hard and cold into Hertford's hand, and the secretary, glancing down, saw the blue nose of an automatic protruding from between his fingers. Barrington turned to the manager.

'Now,' he said, crisply, 'will you kindly show me where the man is?'

Wiping the beads of perspiration from his forehead with a white silk handkerchief, the manager turned and trotted off, followed by the scientist.

They descended a flight of stone stairs, and presently came to a corridor lit coldly with electric bulbs which hung from the centre of the concrete roof. The floor was also of concrete, and lining the walls were great steel doors, the lights from the roof shining on the heavy brass handles and dials that controlled the combination locks.

The manager halted and pointed to where, near the end of the passage, one of the doors stood slightly ajar and through which streamed a ray of light. 'He is in there,' he whispered nervously. 'I won't come any further if — '

Barrington nodded, and held up his hand to enjoin silence. Then, silently, noiselessly, he commenced to creep down the corridor in the direction of the half-open door.

As he reached it, a slight sound like a click of metal against metal came to his ears. Barrington slipped his hand into his pocket and withdrew his other automatic, pressing back the safety catch. He peered round the corner of the great steel door.

A single electric torch glowed from the roof of the small steel-lined cell-like room, and its light revealed that the steel shelves which surrounded the apartment were empty. The only item in the safe was a large polished steel box above two feet square. Bending over this, and in the act of inserting something into a tiny hole in the top of the box, was the figure of a man. Barrington recognised him instantly. It was the man addressed as Doctor by his companion at Margrave Street. His back was half turned to the scientist, but some instinct — a sort of sixth sense — must have warned him that he was being watched, for suddenly he turned round quickly and looked up, and at the same instant Barrington stepped into the safe-like room and covered him with his automatic.

'Doctor Manning, I believe,' he said, smiling grimly. 'I'm afraid I shall have to request you to put your hands above your head.'

'My heavens! Eustace Barrington!' gasped the man, raising his hands.

'And the very last person you expected to see, I've no doubt,' murmured the scientist, 'after the very pleasant little reception — I might almost call it house-warming — that you prepared for me at Margrave Street.'

Doctor Maiming remained silent; then,

as Barrington advanced a step, he suddenly raised his foot and kicked sharply. The toe of his shoe caught the professor a shattering blow on his wrist, and the weapon flew from his hand. At the same instant, the doctor hurled himself upon the scientist and bore him with a crash to the floor.

Barrington was for the moment taken completely unawares. The whole thing had happened so swiftly that he found himself on the ground almost before he realised what had taken place. The doctor's strong claw-like fingers were about his throat, and the professor strove in vain to loosen that strangling grip. The savage kick on his wrist had numbed his arm, so that it was practically useless. As the steel-like hold contracted about his throat, a red mist swam before his eyes, and the blood surged and hammered in his head like a maelstrom.

Tensing his muscles suddenly, Barrington shot up both his knees, at the same time twisting over on to his side. He caught the man above him right in the small of the back with the force of a battering ram, and with a gasp of pain, the doctor for a second released his deadly hold on the scientist's throat. It was only for an instant, but it was sufficient for Barrington; with an eel-like twist he wriggled free. But Doctor Manning was quicker. As he relaxed his fingers from the professor's throat, he sprang to his feet, and snatching up Barrington's automatic from where it had fallen on the floor, made a bound for the door.

Suddenly realising his intention, Barrington hurled himself forward, but he was too late. Even as he did so, the doctor sprang across the threshold and slammed the heavy steel door in the scientist's face. The only hope now was Hertford, for Barrington knew that he was virtually a prisoner, with no hope of getting out until someone arrived with a key that fitted that particular safe.

To Bobbie, waiting above, the seconds passed on leaden feet, and more than once he was tempted to leave his post and try to find out what was happening below. But the professor had told him to remain where he was, and on these occasions Bobbie Hertford always obeyed orders implicitly.

Suddenly he heard a cry from the direction in which Barrington had followed the manager. It was followed by a sharp crack — the sound of an automatic.

Hertford spun round as a tall man, who the secretary recognised even in that brief instant as one of the men he had followed from the house on North Side to Margrave Street, came racing towards him. He sprang forward to intercept him, but the man, holding an automatic pistol by the barrel, dealt him a tremendous blow on the point of the chin. A curtain of crimson before his eyes, Hertford crumpled up without a sound, in an inanimate heap.

He recovered his senses to find Eustace Barrington and the manager bending over him. He sat up, tenderly feeling his jaw. 'What — what happened, sir?' he asked shakily, as with the assistance of the scientist, he staggered to his feet.

Eustace Barrington's face was grim. 'He got away, Hertford,' he said, and briefly recounted what had happened.

'I'm sorry, sir,' said Bobbie. 'My hat! That was some blow!' He felt his chin gently. Barrington patted him on the shoulder.

'You couldn't help it, my boy, any more than I could.' He turned to the manager, who was standing by, white and decidedly shaky. 'Can I use your telephone?' he asked. The manager nodded, and led the way into his office. In a few moments, Barrington got through to Scotland Yard, and was speaking to Inspector Evens.

'Have you had any report from your man who was watching the house on North Side?' asked the scientist after he had informed Evens what had occurred. 'I don't for an instant suppose that Manning will go back there, but it would be as well to send some men down on the off chance. In the meanwhile, will you come along here at once?'

The gruff voice of the inspector replied that he would be along immediately, and Barrington hung up the receiver.

'Now,' he said, turning to the manager, 'I'd like to go back to that safe.'

Accompanied by Hertford, they returned along the concrete corridor to the little safe-like room. Beyond the fact that his jaw ached terribly, the secretary had almost recovered his usual form. Barrington stood for moment at the entrance to the safe and surveyed the interior; then he advanced into the room and, dropping to his knees, commenced a close search of the steel-lined floor. The manager watched with unfeigned astonishment, but Hertford gave a shrewd guess as to what his employer was looking for.

Suddenly the scientist pounced upon something in one corner of the floor, and rose to his feet. Hertford saw that he held between his long fingers a small object that flashed in the light from the electric bulb in the roof. It was a little steel ball. The professor twisted it about between his fingers and then went over to the polished steel box which occupied the centre of the room. For some minutes he stood looking at it, while Hertford and the manager watched him with interest.

The box was beautifully made, apparently of solid steel. About three-quarters of the way up its sides ran a faint line right round it, evidently where the lid opened from the lower half of the box, but so perfectly fitting was it that the joint was barely perceptible. In the top of the box were two tiny round holes, one at each of the front corners. They were not quite round however, for in one were five little nicks and in the other six, giving them somewhat the appearance of tiny stars. Eustace Barrington bent forward. As he did so, there came the sound of approaching feet along the corridor, and a clerk arrived, followed by the burly form of Detective Inspector Evens.

The professor straightened up as the inspector appeared in the doorway. 'Well, Evens,' he said, turning and facing the Scotland Yard man, 'I'm glad you've come. I think I can show you something that will interest you.'

Evens tipped his hard bowler hat further back on his bullet head. 'What is it, Professor?' he grunted as he eyed the steel box and the little ball in the scientist's fingers. 'What did you want me for? Pity the man got away — great pity!'

Harrington nodded. 'It couldn't be helped,' he said. 'I admit that it was my fault, but we'll get him yet. In the meantime, there's one consolation. He escaped empty-handed. He failed to get away with what he came for.'

'What did he come for?' asked Evens.

'The contents of this steel box,' replied Harrington, laying his hand upon it. 'If my theory is correct, this box holds a considerable fortune — close on three quarters of a million.' He bent over the box as Evens stepped forward to his side. 'You see those two tiny star-shaped holes in the top?' He indicated them with his forefinger. 'According to my theory, it requires the insertion of the two little steel balls, one of which I found in Lessard's tooth and the other which, I believe, was concealed in the tooth extracted from Brennan, into those holes to effect the opening of the box. In other words, I believe the principle is on the lines of an automatic machine. Manning, I'm convinced, had already inserted one, and was in the act of dropping in the other when I surprised him.

'Anyhow, we can soon put my idea to the test. If what I believe is correct, I think you'll receive a surprise. The right-hand one of these little openings has five nicks in it, the left-hand one six. The little ball which I hold in my fingers has five tiny projections, so it evidently belongs to the right-hand hole.'

As he spoke, Barrington bent forward and dropped the steel ball into the right-hand hole. Hertford and Inspector Evens came closer, watching with interest. The scientist turned the little steel ball round until the tiny protuberances on its surface corresponded with the nicks in the hole in the box. With a faint rattling sound, the ball disappeared from view. There followed a pause, and then came a faint click. The lid of the box, working on a spring, jerked open about two inches.

Eustace Barrington inserted his firm fingers in the space between the lid and the lower part of the box, and slowly raised the heavy lid. And as he did so, Evens and Hertford gave vent to a gasp of amazement. The light from the roof shone full into the open box, and was reflected a thousandfold from the mass of living fire which poured from its interior.

The scientist peered into the box for a second, and then picked something out and held it up between his finger and thumb: something that flashed and sparkled and radiated countless points of radiant flame. It was a diamond almost as large as a walnut!

Detective Inspector Evens gazed at it in blank surprise, his face alight with excitement. 'My heavens, Professor!' he almost shouted; 'it's the Vandevere Star!'

Barrington smiled quietly as he pointed to the other contents of the steel box. 'And there, my dear Evens,' he murmured softly, 'unless I am very much mistaken, is the rest of the famous Vandevere collection which was stolen from the Vandevere Hall five years ago!'

13

At Yellow Batt's

Professor Barrington was in an irritable mood. It was three days after the discovery of the Vandevere diamonds — three days during which Scotland Yard had searched diligently for some trace of the mysterious Doctor Manning, but without any result. He had completely disappeared.

Frost, the man put to watch the house on North Side, had followed the doctor on the morning he left for the Safe Deposit, but had lost sight of him at the Tube station at Clapham Common, and had failed to pick up his trail again.

Eustace Barrington and Evens, on leaving Waterloo Street, set out at once for 48, but as Barrington expected, they found it deserted. Although they searched every nook and corner of the place, there was not the vestige of a clue by which they could hope to trace Doctor Manning's whereabouts.

In the sitting-room, the professor discovered a mass of burnt paper in the grate, which gave the impression that in any case the occupants of the house had been preparing for flight, but it had been almost entirely destroyed, and only one tiny corner of a card remained unburned. This bore in a pencil scrawl the figures 'one' and 'four', followed by the letters E.A., and apparently was part of an address, but all the rest of the card was so charred that the remainder was indistinguishable. Although the scientist pondered over it for some considerable time, he could make nothing tangible at all out of it. Eustace Barrington, however, never allowed the smallest detail, be it ever so trivial, to be lost, so he had carefully placed the scrap in his pocketbook.

A visit to the estate agent who had charge of the letting of 48 resulted in precisely nothing. The house had been let furnished to Doctor Manning for six months, the owners having gone abroad, and he had, in lieu of the usual references, paid the rent in advance, giving out that he had only recently arrived in London and knew nobody. The agent had never seen the doctor personally, all the business transactions having been conducted by a man calling himself Percival Hastings, who said he was the doctor's secretary. A description of this man convinced Barrington that it was the same man who Hertford had followed from Welbeck Street, and who had held the short conversation with Manning in the room at the house in Margrave Street.

Apparently something had also happened to warn this individual that things had gone wrong; possibly he had been in the vicinity of the Safe Deposit, and had seen the flight of his confederate. At any rate, he had also vanished, and all the threads seemed, one after another, to have broken and for the time, at least, were at a dead end.

Inspector Evens had had a description of the man calling himself Percival Hastings circulated throughout the country, but so far no news had been received. There was no description of Manning, for apparently no one had ever seen him clearly enough to be able to give one. He was merely a name, an enigma, and his real identity remained, like himself, shrouded in mystery. Even when Barrington had confronted him at the Safe Deposit, his face had been half hidden in the folds of the white silk muffler he had been wearing, and the detective's only recollection of him was a pair of singularly piercing dark eyes and a large Roman nose.

Barrington was certain, however, that he would be able to recognise the man again directly he saw him. The doctor's savage attack on Hertford had been so swift in its effect that the secretary had not had time to get more than a vague and hazy idea of his assailant. During his interview with Atherstone, the manager, he had kept the muffler close up, completely concealing the lower part of his face. All the professor's most painstaking inquiries had led to absolutely nothing. Both he and Hertford had simply worked round in a circle, coming inevitably back to the point from which they had started.

This seeming failure and the feeling of absolute impotence had preyed on the scientist's nerves until they were reduced to shreds, and his temper by now was not of the best. He blamed himself entirely for Manning's escape from the Safe Deposit, and he hated the thought that he had blundered. He knew he should have been prepared for Manning's trick.

Up and down the study at Welbeck Street, Eustace Barrington paced ceaselessly, twisting his ring, and utterly oblivious of his surroundings, answering Bobbie's occasional remarks with a grunted monosyllable and refusing all food. Mrs. Timpson had once ventured to remonstrate on this latter part, but Barrington had swung round on the poor old soul with such a look that she had retired hastily to her sitting-room, convinced in her own mind that Master Eustace, as he always remained to her, was on the point of insanity, if not already dangerously mad.

Hertford was very restless, too, but from an entirely different cause. The secretary knew that if the professor went on like this, they would never get any lectures prepared, and the world at large was interested in Professor Barrington the scientist.

'Why don't you try to get some rest, sir?' he ventured at last during the afternoon of the third day, when the professor had suddenly risen from his chair and recommenced his patrol of the study. 'You'll make yourself ill if you go on like this.'

The scientist stopped in his walk and swung round.

'Nonsense,' he snapped. 'A man who spends the greater part of his life trying to elucidate the riddles of the universe shouldn't have any difficulty in solving a small thing like this. Manning can't have vanished into air. He must be somewhere, and I'm going to find him, if I have to spend the rest of my life in the search.' He crossed to the table, and choosing a cigar, lit it with a hand that trembled slightly.

Hertford relapsed into silence. He knew that on an occasion like this, it was useless to argue. Barrington would continue like this until he had hit upon some solution to the problem. The spell of cold weather had been succeeded by a sudden change, and it was much warmer, but the warmth had brought with it rain, and outside in Welbeck Street a nasty thin drizzle was falling, which enhanced the feeling of intense depression that pervaded the atmosphere of the study. Bobbie felt as if some black ominous cloud had descended upon the whole room, blotting out its usual air of cosiness and comfort.

Feeling utterly miserable, and being quite unable to alter the circumstances that produced that feeling, the secretary tried to banish his gloom in work. For some time he sat sorting out documents, and it was only when he discovered that he was putting them under the wrong classification and causing a huge muddle that he came to the conclusion that the work was not having the effect he desired. Shutting the papers up in the drawers of the desk, he sat on the settee and settled down to stare drearily into the fire.

A sudden exclamation from the professor caused Bobbie to look up at his employer sharply. The scientist had paused in his ceaseless tramping and was rummaging among the papers in his desk. He picked up the small piece of charred card which he had found in the house on North Side, and gazed at it for a long moment. Then he suddenly dashed his clenched fist into the palm of his hand. 'By all the signs of the Zodiac, what a fool I am!' he exclaimed.

Hertford sprang to his feet. 'What is it, sir?' he asked. 'Have you discovered anything fresh?'

The scientist's face was changed now: the restless look had gone, and under the shaggy eyebrows his eyes were gleaming with suppressed excitement. 'I've been wasting time, my boy,' he answered. 'Here we've been searching for a clue, and all the time it's been practically in my hand.' He held up the scrap of card. 'I naturally thought that 14 and the letters E.A. were some part of an address — 14 something street — the name of the street being East Street.'

'Well, what are they?' asked Hertford eagerly.

'A telephone number,' replied Barrington.

'I ought to have thought of it immediately, seeing that it's a telephone number we both know. Unless I'm very much mistaken, EA are the first two letters of the word 'East', and 14 the last two numbers in Double two, one four. Now the telephone number East, Double two, one four is — '

'Yellow Batt's,' broke in Hertford excitedly.

'Exactly. One of the worst haunts in the East End, as you and I know very well. Our mysterious doctor friend, Manning, is probably a habitué of the place, and had scrawled down the number at some time or other in order to have it at hand should occasion require it, and destroyed it with his other papers when he decided to leave 48. Also, my boy, don't forget that Yellow Batt was a great friend of Radiant Keller, the man believed originally to have stolen the Vandevere diamonds.'

'I've been waiting to ask you, sir,' said Bobbie, 'how in the world they got into the Safe Deposit, and — '

'I'll answer all your questions at the

right time,' interposed the professor. 'Just now, we haven't any time to lose.' He glanced at his watch. 'Get into some sort of disguise, Bobby — a street loafer will be the best.' He crossed to the door as he spoke and opened it. 'And slip an automatic in your pocket,' he added, pausing on the threshold. 'It's as well to take precautions.'

In the difficult art of disguise, Eustace Barrington was a past master. Not only did he succeed in effectually changing his features and appearance, but by some extraordinary means his whole being changed, so that he literally became the very ego of the character he was representing. All traces of his own strong personality were lost, and every gesture, every action, was perfectly in accord with those of the type he was temporarily impersonating. Barrington might have been a great actor had he so chosen, instead of the great scientist that he was.

Changing swiftly from the blue lounge suit he was wearing to one that was shapeless and of no particular colour, save that it was of some dark material which was very nearly indistinguishable under the layers of grease and grime which covered it, the scientist seated himself before the great mirror in his bedroom and proceeded to make up.

Swiftly and surely, his hands moved along the bottles and paints and collections of cosmetics on the table before him. A tiny piece of wax in each nostril completely altered the shape of his nose. A line here and there, drawn in with the certain deft touch of the artist, and Eustace Barrington swiftly vanished, and in his place there appeared, line by line, and piece by piece, a typical denizen of the underworld: dirty, disreputable, with a sensual leering face, the expression of which would have been enough to have secured him six months in any police court in England. As the professor finished and slipped into a threadbare jacket, the elbows torn and ragged, and pulled a greasy cap over one eye, the door opened and Hertford entered.

'Will this do, sir?' he asked, standing just inside the doorway.

The professor swept him from head to

foot in one sharp, keen glance. The secretary's disguise was simple but effective: he was the embodiment of the usual East End lounger, shabbily, but to a certain extent, flashily dressed, and laden with a quantity of cheap imitation jewellery.

'That's all right, Bobbie,' said his employer approvingly, and he took a final look at himself in the glass before switching out the light in the bedroom and going back to the study. From a drawer in his desk he took an automatic, and having made sure that the mechanism was working properly, slipped it into his hip pocket, together with a fresh clip of cartridges.

'Now we'll be off,' said Barrington, and hurrying down the stairs, they left the house and proceeded down Welbeck Street. A little way along the road, a taxi was slowly crawling, plying for hire, and Barrington hailed it. The driver at first refused to have anything to do with them, which was a tribute to their disguise; but the sight of a Treasury note which the scientist produced soon altered matters, and in a short time while they were bowling along, bound for the East End.

Barrington had instructed the taxi driver to set then down at the Poplar Hippodrome. It was a longish ride, but the professor was so preoccupied with his own thoughts that he scarcely noticed the passing of time, while Hertford was so elated at the idea of action after three days of enforced idleness that he was quite content to sit back in his seat and watch the kaleidoscopic change of scenery as the cab passed rapidly on its way, now passing down a brilliantly lighted street, now taking a short cut through some dim and silent square, and again emerging into the roar and bustle of a main thoroughfare.

Very shortly, the highly respectable shops of the West End gave place to stalls and barrows lit by flaring naphtha lamps and naked electric globes. The hum of well-kept cars and the gentle buzz of conversation of the people on the pavements changed to the clatter of wagons and the raucous shouts of the hawkers displaying their wares on the roadside. A change, too, had taken place in the type of people hurrying along the wet pavements.

Opera cloaks, and their attendant black

dress overcoats, had given place to garish scarves and brilliant hats, soft felt caps and mackintoshes. Presently collars became scarce, and knotted mufflers took their place, while only here and there an overcoat became visible. The bright glaring lights, reflected in the wet gutter, cast a crude, raw radiance over everything, and reminded Hertford of a fairground. People seemed to be moving aimlessly along, with no definite idea of their destination, save that they were going somewhere, and in many places had congregated in little groups at the street corners, laughing and talking, and passing coarse remarks to each other, oblivious alike, or so it seemed, of time and place, and even of the soaking drizzle of rain which still descended without pause or break to throw over the whole scene a damp, misty miasma of sordidness and discomfort.

The cab drew into the kerb at last, and they both alighted, and having paid the driver, proceeded on foot past the Hippodrome.

After going about two hundred yards along the main road, the professor turned off sharply into a dimly lit and evil-smelling alley. He had adopted the usual slouching, dragging step of a habitual lounger, the type of which they often passed.

Through a maze of dark and narrow side streets, they made their way until at last, by the tang in the air, Bobbie could tell that the river was close at hand. They were now in the heart of Pennyfields, that section of the East End which is known as Limehouse, and which breeds more crime and vice than any other part of London, with the exception possibly of Mayfair and a few of the smaller streets that lie behind Leicester Square.

Halfway down a dirty, narrow and uninviting-looking cul-de-sac, the professor and his secretary halted. A distant clock chimed ten. The little street was mostly composed of marine store shops, but opposite to where they had stopped was a laundry. The place was painted a dirty, sickly blue, or looked it in the light of the solitary lamp which was all the illumination the street boasted.

The broken lettering across the filthy

window announced that it was Ling Soo's. This was the place known as Yellow Batt's.

'Be careful, Bobbie,' whispered Barrington as they crossed the road, 'and keep your eyes open.'

He raised his hand and knocked sharply on the grimy panel of the side door — three slow knocks and two quick ones. Eustace Barrington had visited Yellow Batt's before on several occasions, and was well acquainted with the method of obtaining admission. There was a pause, and presently, from behind the door came the sound of a shuffling step. The door opened, and a figure peered out holding a guttering candle. It was a small Chinese man with a parchment-like face badly marked with smallpox.

'East is East,' growled Barrington through one side of his mouth, which is the habitual manner of the class he was impersonating.

'But West and East sometimes meet,' answered the Chinese in a sibilant whisper as he held the door further open. The scientist stepped into the narrow passage, followed by Hertford, and immediately the door was closed. Without another word, the Chinese led the way to the end of the passage, and opened another door.

'Very careful of the stairs,' he warned. Bobbie saw in the light of the flickering candle that a flight of narrow wooden steps led downwards, just inside the door. They were so narrow that they were more like a ladder than a staircase. While the Chinese held the light, the professor and his secretary stumbled down. At the bottom of the stairs, a low-roofed passage turned sharply to the right, and at the end of this was a baize-covered door.

Barrington slouched over to it and pushed it open. A flood of light streamed out, followed by the babel of many voices. The next second the door had closed behind them, and they found themselves inside the establishment of Yellow Batt's.

It was a large, low-ceilinged, cellar-like apartment across one end of which ran a rough bar. Dotted about the place were small folding tables like card tables, the tops of which had been covered with American cloth that had at one time been white, but which was now discoloured with the stains from the dirty bottoms of many glasses and burned with the stumps of countless cigarettes. The place was lit by some dozen or more oil lamps which swung from the blackened ceiling, the light struggling to penetrate through the glass of the smoky, grimy chimneys, and warmth was provided by an iron stove, the escape pipe of which ran up and along the roof and through a hole in the wall beside a second door at the other end of the room.

The place was full of the most heterogeneous cosmopolitan collection of humanity it was possible to imagine. All the flotsam and jetsam of the world seemed to have gathered together under the roof of Yellow Batt's. Seated at the little tables and gathered in chattering groups round the bar were Lascars, Chinese, blacks, Sepoys, every conceivable race and colour, with a plentiful sprinkling of white, some flashily dressed and some down-at-heel ragged loungers, with here and there a stoker or sailor from some merchant vessel in dock for fresh cargo.

The atmosphere of the place was nauseating. The thick haze of tobacco smoke intermingled with the smell of spirits and stale beer, and behind the bar, presiding over the mixed assembly like a king over his subjects, was the proprietor of the establishment — Yellow Batt!

Yellow Batt was an Englishman. He was a tall, well-built man of about sixty, and his face, although fleshy, was of a peculiar yellowish colour, caused by the fact that its owner suffered from jaundice. His hair was snow-white, and he wore it long, brushed straight back from his high forehead so that it fell over his coat collar at the back. Altogether, Yellow Batt possessed a striking personality.

He was well known to the police, and his establishment was regarded as a sort of human cesspool where sooner or later most of the criminals wanted by the police drifted. More 'wanted' men, and women, too, for that matter, had been arrested as they left the cellar-like demesne of Yellow Batt's than anywhere else in London, and it was for this reason that the establishment in Limehouse was allowed to remain open and unmolested by the authorities.

A Chinese man who might have been the twin brother of the one who had admitted Barrington and his secretary was hurrying to and fro, serving drinks. No one took any note of the newcomers as they slouched across to a vacant table and sat down. Having ordered drinks, Eustace Barrington allowed his eyes to wander over the mixed assembly.

There were many present who were well known to the scientist, for his hobby of criminology had often led him into the underworld, and he seldom forgot a face, or the story connected with that particular face. Here at Yellow Batt's, he recognised thieves and cracksmen, petty sneaks and habitual criminals.

Over by the bar, drinking a double whiskey and soda, was a little dark-haired man, rather on the stout side, whom the scientist knew to be a notorious fence.

Had any of the assembly present so much as guessed for an instant that the eminent scientist of Welbeck Street was among them, it is doubtful if his life would have been worth a moment's purchase, for his fame as a criminologist was already known to the underworld. The Chinese man shuffled up with the drinks the Processor had ordered, and Barrington gulped his down, smacking his lips in approval and ordering another. While the man was present, Barrington kept up a running fire of conversation through one side of his mouth, in the approved fashion of the underworld, but as soon as the attendant had departed to carry out his order, he turned to Bobbie.

'We may have to wait some time for developments, my boy,' he whispered, 'and possibly nothing at all will result, but I'm hoping that we may hear something that will give us a clue to the whereabouts of Doctor Manning, for I feel convinced that he jotted down the telephone number of this place with a very definite object in view.'

Hertford nodded. 'Perhaps he was contemplating getting rid of the diamonds through someone here,' he replied in a low voice. 'There's old Zimmerman over there.' His eyes travelled to where the little stout man was leaning up against the bar, talking in low tones to Yellow Batt. 'He's just the sort to handle a big deal like that.'

'I shouldn't be surprised if you were right,' answered Barrington. He pressed his knee warningly against Hertford's as the Chinese man returned with the drink. Waiting until the man had again passed out of hearing, the scientist continued. 'However,' he said, 'all we can do is to watch and wait. It looks to me as though Batt was expecting someone.'

Several times since their arrival, the proprietor of the establishment had glanced at the cheap clock which ticked loudly at the back of the bar, and from it to the baize-covered door which gave ingress into the room. Once or twice it had opened to admit fresh arrivals, but they were apparently not the right ones, for Yellow Batt still retained his watch on the clock and his general air of expectancy. The close atmosphere of the place was beginning to make Hertford's head swim and his eyes smart, and it was getting near to eleven o'clock before anything happened.

The secretary was engaged in looking at the other door, beside which the outlet pipe from the stove passed, and conjecturing where it might lead to, when the sudden quick grasp of Barrington's hand on his knee made him look round sharply. The baize door had opened, and a man had entered the apartment. Yellow Batt caught sight of him, and instantly stopped his conversation with the stout Zimmerman, waving a hand in greeting to the new arrival.

Hertford drew in his breath with a hiss of excitement as he recognised him. It was the man he had followed from Welbeck Street to the house on the North Side!

14

The Chase!

There was no mistaking the wolfish face and perpetually snarling mouth. Hertford could have picked the man out from among a thousand. With a swift glance round the cellar-like room, the newcomer crossed straight over to the bar and commenced to talk quickly in low tones to Yellow Batt, as the latter bent over the counter towards him. The conversation was carried on in whispers, and strain his ears as he might, not a single word could the professor catch. The man appeared to be giving Yellow Batt some instructions of some description, for every now and again the Englishman would nod his head as if to confirm that he understood what the other was saying.

Barrington turned to Bobbie. 'Sit tight, my boy,' he whispered. 'I'm going over to the bar to try and see if I can catch what our friend is talking about.'

He rose to his feet as he spoke, and slouched across the room, carrying his glass in his hand. Elbowing his way among the group of nondescripts who were standing immediately in the vicinity of the new-comer and Yellow Batt, he banged his glass on the counter to attract the attention of the proprietor. Batt stopped his conversation and looked up.

''Ere, I say,' growled Barrington, 'd'yer think I'm goin' to wait all the bloomin' night for a drink?'

'All right, mate,' said Batt. 'Whatcher want?'

'Gimme a double whiskey, and none o' yer watery muck,' said the professor ill-humouredly.

'Not feelin' so well, are yer?' said Batt as he executed the order. 'We don't sell anythink but the best o' stuff 'ere, my lad.'

Barrington growled a reply as the glass was pushed across to him, and he grabbed it, flinging a coin on the counter in payment. Gulping it down and loudly smacking his lips, he called for another, and when this was given to him, remained leaning against the bar.

Yellow Batt resumed his muttered conversation with the man who had last entered. The scientist drew a packet of cigarette papers and some tobacco from his pocket and proceeded to roll a cigarette, straining his ears all the while, to catch the drift of their whispered conference. Their heads were close together, and their voices were so low that he only managed to distinguish a word here and there. ' — not before.' ' — too risky — ' A low murmur followed, then, ' — later tonight . . . by the river — ' Again the voice dropped. ' . . . pick up at Gravesend.'

Yellow Batt asked some questions here, apparently, for the man replied in a slightly louder voice, ' — in the motorboat, of course . . . Manning will — '

Barrington couldn't hear the rest of the sentence, and after this, Yellow Batt left the man to serve some of his disreputable customers who were clamouring for attention. Eustace Barrington waited for some time, and then, draining his glass, returned to the table where he had left Hertford.

'I haven't learnt much,' he said in reply to the questioning look in his secretary's eyes. 'But from what I did hear, and from what I guess, I think that Manning is expected later tonight, probably in a boat from the river. In a moment or two I want you to leave here and go at once to the nearest station of the river police — there's one not far from here, along Limehouse reach — see the inspector in charge, and arrange for a fast launch to be in readiness, and waiting on the opposite bank of the river at the back of Yellow Batt's — tell them to put out all lights on the launch and wait. You'll go with them, and as soon as you hear a shot, you'll make all speed for the back of this side of the river and pick me up. Do you understand, Bobbie?'

Hertford nodded somewhat dubiously. 'But what about you, sir?' he whispered. 'I don't like leaving you here alone like this, and — '

'I shall be all right, my boy,' interposed

the professor. 'Now be off as quickly as you can. We don't know how long we've got before Manning arrives or how long he's going to stop when he does, and I don't want to risk losing him again. Good night, cully,' he added in a louder voice as Hertford rose to his feet. 'See yer in the same 'ole tomorrer.'

'So long, mate,' replied Bobbie. He thrust his hands into the pockets of his trousers, and swaggered across the room to the baize door. He paused for a moment as he opened the door, and waved his hand with a flourish to Barrington before passing through.

After his secretary's departure, the professor remained seated at his table letting his eyes stray over the scene before him. Manning's companion still remained standing by the bar, silently sipping a glass of rum and taking no notice of anyone around him. Every now and then his eyes shot to the clock, but beyond that he remained motionless. Yellow Batt had resumed his conversation with the stout Zimmermann.

Twelve o'clock passed, and half past.

The hands of the clock were creeping towards one when suddenly there came a sharp rap-rap at the door on the opposite side of the cellar. Eustace Barrington's whole being drew tense and alert. Was this what he had been waiting for — the arrival of the mysterious Doctor Manning?

Yellow Batt raised the flap at one end of the counter and crossed the floor to the door. Stopping, he drew a key from his pocket and unlocked and unbolted it. As it swung inwards, a tall muffled figure entered, a slouch hat drawn down close over his eyes. Barrington felt a little thrill of exultation pass through him as he recognised the figure of the man. It was Doctor Manning!

His hat and coat glistened in the light as he advanced into the room, a little trail of water remaining in his wake. Evidently, thought the professor, the rain had increased in violence, and to judge by Manning's appearance, it must now be pouring in torrents.

The mysterious and sinister doctor crossed directly over to his confederate at the bar, and removing his streaming hat, shook it thoroughly on the floor. For the first time, Eustace Barrington obtained a clear view of his face. A large thin nose projected from between a pair of deep-set eyes. Hr had a thin slit of a mouth with tightly compressed lips that were of a peculiar vivid red — too red for a man. The upper lip short, so that it was overshadowed by the heavy nose, and a receding forehead that bulged at the brows and overshadowed the eyes. Such was the repellent face of Dr. Manning. His head was covered with a crop of closely cut iron-grey hair, save where a slight bald patch showed in the centre.

There was something vaguely familiar about him, something which stirred a fugitive memory in Eustace Barrington's brain, but try as he would he could not isolate it, anchor it, and give it a name. He was certain, however, that at some time he had seen that face before, though where, and under what circumstances, he could not at the moment define.

Having shaken as much of the water as possible from his hat, the doctor replaced it upon his head and ordered a glass of hot whiskey and water. Had there been any doubt in the professor's mind — which there was not — as to his identity, the sound of that sharp rasping voice would soon have set it at rest. No one, once having heard Doctor Manning speak, would ever be likely in a hurry to forget the tone of his voice.

The doctor turned to his companion and commenced speaking rapidly in a low tone, accompanying his words with sharp, quick gestures of his hands and head. He appeared to be in a considerably bad temper, and Barrington smiled to himself as he caught the words: ' — that cursed Professor and his confounded meddling,' and guessed the cause of the doctor's ill humour.

For Barrington very well knew that though Manning had escaped from the Safe Deposit, he had got away empty-handed, and all his plotting and scheming had come to nothing. The man was now evidently concentrating all his mind and energy in flight. He was well aware now that all idea of securing the Vandevere diamonds could be set aside as hopeless. His one chance on which he had staked everything had failed, and the chance was not likely to be repeated. The diamonds were now as far away from Doctor Manning as if they had been buried in the middle of the Atlantic.

Barrington sensed the impotent rage that filled the doctor's brain against himself. Zimmerman and Yellow Batt had now joined Manning and the other man, and the whole four were engaged in an animated conversation. Barrington wondered what exactly the doctor's plans were. From the few scraps of information he had gathered from what Manning's companion had been saying to the proprietor of the place, it seemed as though Manning was going to pick something up at Gravesend. But what was it? The professor had hazarded a guess that it meant that the doctor's intention was to travel by the river in a motorboat and board some other boat at Gravesend. Barrington felt pretty sure that his idea was right. Manning, of course, was well aware that the police were keeping a sharp look out for him, and with all his precautions he could not be sure that his description was unknown.

Again that vague elusive memory stirred in Eustace Barrington's brain. Where had he seen the doctor before? Was it in some photograph? His thoughts were suddenly switched back to the present, as he saw Yellow Batt hand a small packet over the bar to Manning. The doctor took it and carefully stowed it away in an inside pocket, and then commenced to button up his overcoat and settled his muffler more closely round his chin. Apparently he was on the point of departure. Barrington rose from his seat and carelessly lounged over to the bar, his brain keen and alert.

He had no intention of allowing the doctor to escape him a second time, but he had to move carefully. Single-handed he was powerless, and he knew only too well that he could expect no help from the habitues of Yellow Batt. His only course was to follow the doctor when he left, and get him outside. Hertford had had ample time to carry out his instructions, and provided Barrington's idea was correct, and Manning had a motorboat outside, he could overtake him in the police launch and catch him on the river. The professor was convinced that he would leave the place as he had entered it — by the door, which he knew opened close to the riverbank. Had he been certain of this in the first place, he could easily have left with Hertford and waited with him in the police launch until Manning came out. But it had only been a conjecture — was only supposition now, although Barrington had a shrewd idea that he was right. But, on the other hand, if he was wrong, and he had left the place, he stood a very real chance of losing Manning for good and all, and Barrington was not taking any risks.

The question that was occupying his mind at the moment was how he could follow the doctor through that door without giving the alarm, and he had to make up his mind quickly, for already Manning was shaking hands with Zimmerman, clearly on the point of leaving. Yellow Batt came out from behind the bar and crossed over to the door, followed by Manning and his companion. He had now unlocked the door, and stood with it partly open, while he shook hands with the doctor.

It was now or never, and Barrington's quick brain had already evolved a scheme. It was hazardous, but he couldn't afford to chance the door being locked again. On the counter by his elbow stood a large oil lamp. He waited until Manning, with a final word, had passed out through the door, and Yellow Batt had cried hoarsely 'Good luck!' and was in the act of closing the door behind him. Then, while the owner of the cellar was searching his pockets for the key to relock the door, the professor acted.

Edging away from the lamp and nearer the exit to the river, he took a swift glance round. No one appeared to be looking in his direction, and stretching out his long arm, the scientist deliberately knocked the lamp off the counter on the floor in front! It fell with a loud clatter, and the oil in the container streamed out over the wooden flooring and burst into flames!

Instantly, as Barrington had hoped, there was a shout, and everyone in the place concentrated their attention on the catastrophe.

With an oath, Yellow Batt left the door and hurried over to the spot where the lamp had fallen.

'Which of you clumsy fools did that?' he roared. A babel of voices answered him, denying knowledge of the accident.

In the confusion, while everyone was engaged in trying to stamp out the flames, Barrington ran to the door and slipped out. As he did so, someone in the crowd behind him saw him go, and raised a shout. But he was through. The back exit of Yellow Batt's led on to a rotting wharf piled with old packing cases, barrels, staved in and useless, and strewn with every conceivable kind of rubbish and lumber. In front of Barrington was a great pile of rusty scrap iron, and from this it was less than fifty yards to the river itself. The scientist was in time to see the tall figure of Doctor Manning disappearing down a rough wooden ladder at the end of the wharf. A sudden burst of sound behind him made the professor turn his head for an instant.

A little crowd headed by the Chinese attendant was pouring through the door by which he had just left. From in front of Barrington came the muffled chug-chug of a motor engine, and he saw a dark shape move away from the wharf and head for mid-tream, gathering speed as it did so. Barrington ducked sharply as some heavy object whizzed past his head and struck the edge of the wharf with a dull thud. The professor felt in his pocket for his automatic, breaking into a run as he did so. He knew that the men behind him dared not risk shooting. The noise was too likely to attract the attention of the police, and that was the very last thing that Yellow Batt and his satellites desired. Barrington raised his pistol and fired one shot in the air.

At the same instant, he felt a sharp pain in his left arm as something brushed by his sleeve. Someone behind had thrown a knife! A quick glance back showed him that the Chinese man was now not more than ten yards to his rear. Barrington had reached the end of the wharf by now, and the faint sound of a motor engine coming rapidly nearer reached his ears. It must be Hertford in the police launch, in answer to his signal. The professor paused for a second on the edge of the wharf; then, making up his mind, dived off into the river just as the crowd behind burst onto the jetty.

He rose to the surface gasping, for the water was very cold. A shower of missiles fell all round him as he did so, but luckily none hit him, and he struck out for the sound of the motor engine. Suddenly a dark shadow loomed up in front of Barrington. He gave a cry, and heard Hertford's voice shouting excitedly as the noise of the engine ceased, and the next moment he was being dragged on board by his secretary and a constable.

'Quickly!' gasped Harrington through his chattering teeth. 'After that motorboat that went down the river just now. Don't lose it, whatever you do. Manning's in it!'

'I was getting anxious, sir,' said Bobbie as he handed the professor a heavy coat to wrap himself in, and helped him into the tiny shelter just behind the bows of the launch. 'When the time went by, and Inspector Elmore and I heard nothing, I began to think that something had gone wrong.'

'Ah, it's you, Elmore, is it?' said Barrington, as he grasped the inspector's hand. 'I suppose Hertford here told you who we're after?'

Elmore, a jovial, stout man, nodded his head. 'Yes, Professor,' he replied, grasping the side of the shelter as the motorboat veered sharply round and went tearing off down the river like a greyhound released from its leash, a fountain of spray dashing up over the bows. 'We shall catch him all right; this is one of the fastest boats on the river.'

Barrington smiled grimly, his eyes fixed upon the darkness ahead. Manning's boat, like the pursuing launch, carried no lights, and it had got a fairly good start. At the moment there was not a sign of it, but the night was dark, and it was impossible to see very far in front. The rain was still streaming down, and this still further tended to obscure the view.

They had now reached Blackwall Reach, and were racing on in the direction of Woolwich. In spite of the coat which Hertford had somehow managed to find for him, Barrington was shivering with the cold, his clothes clinging clammily to his body.

Suddenly Hertford, who was gazing eagerly ahead, grasped his employer's shoulder. 'There they are, sir!' he cried excitedly.

The scientist peered out in front, through the mist of mingled spray and rain. After a second or two, he made out a vague shadow ahead; a rapidly moving smudge upon the dark surface of the waters.

'By Jove! They're speeding!' he said, turning to the inspector. 'Are we going as fast as we can, Elmore? They'll beat us at this rate.'

Inspector Elmore left his side and shouted something to the man at the wheel. Barrington could not hear what he said, for his voice was caught and carried away by the rush of air past the launch. But as if in answer, the boat quivered like a living thing and literally seemed to hurl itself through the water, which swept past on each side like two walls of frosted glass.

On, on tore the launch, past Woolwich, through Halfway Reach, and still on towards Erith and Wennington March; but still the boat in front kept its lead. Barrington in his excitement had forgotten his wet condition and, discarding the overcoat, was standing up peering ahead, his eyes fixed on the fleeing motorboat containing Doctor Manning.

'Ye Gods!' exclaimed Bobbie. 'That boat's got some engine!'

Barrington nodded, his eyes still staring intently away into the darkness over the spray-swept bows of the launch. 'We're not gaining an inch,' he muttered in vexation. 'At this rate, I'm afraid they'll outdistance us.'

Inspector Elmore came up behind him in time to hear the professor's last words. 'We've crammed on all the speed we can, sir,' he said anxiously. 'I can't get another inch out of her. Jupiter! That boat's a goer! There's another thing, too, that's troubling me. We're running short of petrol.'

Eustace Barrington swung round in dismay. This was an emergency he had not bargained for. 'How long can we keep going?' he asked.

'Not more than another quarter of an hour,' answered Elmore. 'I'd no idea we were in for a long trip, or I'd have had some spare cans put on board.'

The professor clenched his hands unconsciously. Was Manning going to beat him after all? They were passing Purfleet now, and heading straight for the Dartford Marshes and —

A cry from Hertford broke in on Barrington's thoughts and once more sent his eyes in the direction of the boat ahead.

'Look, sir. Look!' cried the boy excitedly. 'I'm sure we're gaining!'

Barrington and Elmore peered eagerly forward. Bobbie was right! The distance between the two racing boats had appreciably lessened. The police launch was gaining on its quarry inch by inch. Suddenly from the boat in front came a confused intermittent crackling, replacing the rhythmic chug-chug of a moment before.

'He's having engine trouble,' shouted Elmore. 'It's misfiring! If it continues, we've got a good chance of catching the blighters after all. If the petrol'll only hang out long enough.'

Gradually the launch was eating up the intervening space between itself and the boat it was pursuing. Then out of the darkness in front came a sudden stab of flame, followed by a sharp whip-like report. There was a dull thud as a bullet buried itself in one of the wooden supports of the shelter behind which Barrington and Hertford and the inspector were standing. Manning had evidently realised that they were overtaking him, and had started shooting.

Crack! Again came the report, and Barrington felt the wind of the bullet this time as it flew past the side of the shelter by which he was standing. The scientist's hand sought his own automatic, and he was in the act of drawing it when he realised that his immersion in the river must have rendered the weapon useless.

Crack! Crack! A veritable fusillade of shots came from the boat in front, and with a cry, the man at the wheel of the police launch clapped his hand to the side of his head and collapsed in the bottom of the boat. The launch gave a sudden lurch as the helm spun round, and it swerved out of its course and raced for the bank. The jolt threw Elmore and Hertford off their feet, but Barrington by a supreme effort kept his balance and made a leap for the wheel. Spinning it round, he once more set the launch in a straight course, but the delay had increased the distance between the boats. Hertford staggered up, and regaining his feet, drew his automatic and emptied its contents into the boat in front.

One of the bullets must have hit some vital part of the steering gear, for the motorboat suddenly zigzagged for a yard or two and then, turning sharply, almost at right angles, crashed heavily into the riverbank.

Eustace Barrington, with a twist of the wheel, sent the launch veering round, and stopped as it buried its bows in the soft mud of the bank scarcely a yard from where the other boat had struck. As he leapt out, followed by Elmore and Bobbie, his feet sank in the muddy ooze of the marshland. Two or three yards ahead he saw the figure of Manning staggering along, his feet sinking in the soft slimy ground at every step. He turned once, and seeing Barrington behind him, raised his automatic and fired at the professor, but he ducked and the bullet passed harmlessly over his head. It must have been the last shot in the magazine, for Manning flung away his pistol and continued on his way.

It was heavy going, for the soft mud clung to their feet, and it was like wading through treacle; but Barrington kept on, and slowly but surely was overtaking his prey. He was less than five yards behind Manning when the latter stumbled forward and disappeared up to his knees. He had slipped into a deep depression in the soft marshy ground, full of half-liquid mud. The next second Barrington was level with him, and, leaning forward, had gripped the man by the shoulder. Manning tried to shake himself free, but the scientist's grip was like a steel vice, and with his legs clogged by the clinging slime, the doctor was powerless to escape. Hertford and Elmore arrived at that moment, and the boy directed the beams of his torch on Barrington and his prisoner.

From under the brim of his soft hat, Manning shot a malevolent glance at the scientist, his lips parted in a snarl of impotent fury. Elmore caught him by the other arm, and with the assistance of Barrington, dragged him out of the tenaciously clinging mud on to the comparatively firmer ground of the marsh, and the next minute had snapped the handcuffs on the doctor's wrists.

'Phew, Mr. Barrington,' panted the inspector, wiping his forehead with his handkerchief. 'It's hard work running through this confounded slush.'

The professor seemed scarcely to hear him. In that single second when Manning had glared up at him, the elusive memory that had haunted him earlier in the evening had all at once become a sharp and clear image, and he remembered now where it was he had seen the doctor's face before. Then he forced his mind back to the present.

'What about the man who was with him?' he asked.

'He's safe enough,' answered Hertford. 'He's lying by the boat with a broken leg.'

'We'd better get back to the launch. I expect there'll be enough petrol in Manning's boat to run us as far as the nearest river police station.'

With the doctor between him and Inspector Elmore, they floundered their way back to the launch. Manning had never once opened his tightly compressed lips, but his eyes were fixed on the scientist with an expression that boded ill for Barrington had he been free and in possession.

Manning's companion lay groaning on the bank beside the half-overturned boat as they approached, and by the light of Hertford's torch they saw that one leg was curiously bent under him; evidently the shock of the impact had thrown him violently out, and his leg, sticking in the mud, had been broken. Near to his hand lay an automatic.

As gently as possible, Hertford and the inspector carried him to the launch, while Barrington followed with Manning. They found the mechanic who had been driving the police boat on the point of recovering consciousness. The bullet had only grazed the side of his head, but it had been sufficient to stun him for the time being.

Having got their prisoners on board, Bobbie went in search of petrol and discovered a spare can in the other boat, and also a suitcase, both of which he transferred to the launch. A few seconds later, they were speeding up the river in the direction from whence they had come. Manning sat sullenly quiet, crouched in one corner of the shelter, his manacled hands hanging loosely between his knees. Only once he spoke, and that was when Inspector Elmore touched his shoulder as they drew near their destination.

As he rose to his feet, he turned towards Barrington. 'Curse you, you damned amateur. Why can't you keep to your own job?' he snarled, a world of hatred smouldering in his deep-set eyes. 'The police would never have got me, and but for you I — '

'Here! That's enough of that!' broke in Elmore, catching him by the arm.

The doctor swung round on him, and Hertford sprang to his feet. For a moment, he thought Manning was about to attack the inspector. But by a supreme effort of will, the doctor choked back his rage and shrugged his shoulders.

And Eustace Barrington, looking on quietly and catching sight of the expression on the man's face, realised that in the capture of Doctor Manning he had rid the civilised world of a particularly dangerous personality.

15

The Professor Explains

The study at Welbeck Street presented a particularly cosy appearance on the evening following the capture of Doctor Manning on the Dartford Marshes.

Outside, the rain splashed and pattered on the window panes as though jealous of the comfort within, and in the chimney the voice of the wind howled dismally as the roaring fire growlingly refused it admittance.

Seated round the fire, where they had congregated after an excellent dinner, were five people. They consisted of the professor; Detective Inspector Evens; Moira Lessard; the young lawyer, Wallace Manton; and last, but by no means least — the professor's young secretary, Bobbie Hertford.

The red, jovial face of Evens glistened in the firelight, for by mutual consent they had not switched on the electrics, and the worthy inspector looked at peace with the whole world. At his elbow stood a glass of Barrington's famous old port, and in his short stubby fingers was one of the scientist's excellent cigars.

Barrington lay back in his favourite armchair, his massive well-poised head and virile body for once at rest. Having received permission from Moira Lessard, who was herself smoking a cigarette which Wallace Manton had offered her, Barrington chose a cigar, and the men lit up.

The young lawyer had called that morning, and the scientist, who guessed the interest the young man felt for Mrs. Lessard, had invited him to be present at the little dinner he was giving at Welbeck Street that night to celebrate the successful conclusion of the problem. He was seated now upon the big chesterfield drawn up in front of the fire, beside Hertford, his eyes scarcely ever leaving the figure of Moira Lessard, who occupied the armchair opposite Barrington. She looked very young and beautiful as she sat, leaning forward, her eyes fixed with a look of expectancy on the professor. She was wearing a simple evening frock of black, and its ebony shade threw into relief the rounded whiteness of her neck and shoulders, while the flickering light of the fire played upon the soft, fair, curling hair which, in the prevailing fashion, was cut close to her shapely head. Hertford grinned to himself as with a sidelong glance, he caught the look in the young lawyer's eyes as they rested upon her.

At the beginning of dinner, Barrington had been bombarded with questions from all sides concerning the case, but the scientist had resolutely refused to answer a single one of them until after the conclusion of the meal. The others, although inwardly bursting with curiosity, had respected their host's whim, and the conversation had relapsed into generalities. Barrington was a brilliant talker when he chose, and a great psychologist, and he kept his guests amused with a flow of anecdotes and witty epigrams until at his suggestion they had adjourned to the study for coffee.

Having seen that his guests were all

contentedly smoking, he knew that the right moment had arrived for him to tell his story.

Evens turned to him. 'Now, Barrington,' he grunted in a voice that was intended to be genial, but which sounded like a playful bear with a very bad cold, 'when you've finished giving an excellent imitation of an oyster, perhaps you'll relieve our curiosity concerning the case, for I'm still in the dark as to the meaning of it all.'

'I think we're all very anxious, Professor, to hear your explanation,' said Moira.

Barrington smiled quietly, and settled himself more comfortably in his chair whilst his right hand felt for and found his ring. 'This case,' he began at last, 'is one that illustrates to a marked degree the vital connection between cause and effect. In other words, it can be divided into two entirely separate and distinct parts. The first part, which is a complete story on its own, represents the cause from which the events that constitute the second part, or effect side of the case, sprang.'

Barrington paused for a moment and slowly twisted the ring three times round his finger. The others were listening intently, hanging on every word that dropped from the scientist's lips. After a moment he continued.

'In order to fully understand the sequence of events that constitute the main items of the mystery surrounding the murder of the two Lessards and the subsequent killing of Brennan in the grounds of Copthorn House, it is necessary to go back about five years previously to the dates on which these events occurred.

'About that time, there was perpetrated at Vandevere Hall a singularly audacious robbery. Sir Maurice Vandevere, as some of you are probably aware, was the possessor of a wonderful collection of diamonds, among which was the famous stone known as the Vandevere Star, considered to be the second largest diamond in the world. This collection was housed in a specially built strong room which Sir Maurice had had constructed at Vandevere Hall.

'One morning it was discovered that the place had been broken into during the night, and the lock of the strong room melted out with Thermite, and the entire collection stolen. The thieves had left no trace whatever, and the police were absolutely baffled. I myself took a considerable interest in the affair at the time, although I was not asked to elucidate the mystery. The papers were full of it, and for some time it was the sole topic of conversation. Sir Maurice offered a large reward for any information that would lead to the recovery of the stones, but without result.

'The suspicions of the police were centred upon a man named Amos Keller. This man was a noted jewel thief, and had served several terms of imprisonment; in fact, he had only been released from prison about six months prior to the robbery. Added to this, it was known that he specialised entirely in diamonds, a fact which had earned for him the sobriquet of Radiant Keller at the Yard. But although they possessed a strong suspicion that Keller was responsible for the robbery of the Vandevere collection, and although he was religiously watched, the police were unable to unearth a scrap of evidence against him sufficient to arrest him.

'Radiant Keller was provided with an unshakable alibi, and proved conclusively that on the night the burglary had been perpetrated he was playing cards until a late hour with some friends, including a certain Adolf De Castro, at the latter's flat in Notting Hill. It was apparently impossible, therefore, that he could have been concerned in the robbery, as Vandevere Hall is situated on the borders of Dartmoor, and it was humanly impossible that Keller could have covered the distance from London in the time. I say apparently, because I've discovered just lately that Keller's alibi was a fake and a tissue of lies from beginning to end, and he did actually commit the burglary for which he was suspected.

'Now, for some time I had held a theory that, although Radiant Keller worked alone, his was not the brain that planned the coups with which his name was associated, and this theory has lately received startling confirmation. Every theft with which Keller was connected was planned in the first place by a man who remained unknown and unsuspected in the background, the man who arranged his alibi — Adolf De Castro. Against De Castro there was not a breath of suspicion, and on the few occasions when Keller had been caught and arrested, it was to his advantage, for obvious reasons, not to disclose the identity of his confederate.

'The Vandevere robbery was by far the most ambitious of their ventures, for the value of the collection was estimated at something round about three quarters of a million. Whether the enormous amount at stake won the cupidity of Radiant Keller, or whether he suddenly came to the conclusion that as he took all the risk, he was entitled to a larger share in the proceeds, we shall never be able to discover for certain.

'However, it's sufficient to know that for some reason, Keller decided to retain the whole of the Vandevere collection for himself, and not to split it up with De Castro at all.

'Keller had for many years rented a safe at the Safe Deposit in Victoria Street, a fact which was well known to De Castro, in the name of Peter Dale, and this appeared to him to offer an excellent hiding place for the stolen diamonds. De Castro, he knew, was a dangerous man, and at the slightest suspicion that Keller was trying to double-cross him, would stick at nothing to secure his revenge. Therefore, Radiant Keller had to take infinite precautions. He explained to De Castro that he'd deposited the stones at the Safe Deposit, and that it was safer to let them lie there until after the sensation caused by their theft had subsided and the suspicions of the police had been laid at rest. It would be some considerable time before it would be safe to remove such a well-known collection for disposal, and in the meantime they were quite secure. Adolf De Castro was perfectly satisfied with this explanation, which was, by the way, a perfectly true one.

'The most important part, however, Keller had suppressed. Although De Castro knew that he rented a safe at the Deposit, he was entirely unaware in what name Keller held it. In order, however, to make absolutely certain that no one but himself could obtain access to the diamonds, Radiant Keller had constructed a special box of tempered steel, the only way of opening which was by means of two tiny steel balls dropped into two small holes in the lid. The principle was an elaboration of the idea of the ordinary automatic machine, the tiny steel points on the surface of the balls engaging in the wards of the lock as they fell. Having reached this stage in his scheme, Keller took a still further precaution.

'He arranged with the manager of the Safe Deposit that no one, not even himself, was to be admitted to the vault without first producing the two steel balls as a sign of his bonafides, but that anyone who complied with the demand was to be allowed access to it without further question. Having arranged everything to his satisfaction, Radiant Keller, about two weeks later, suddenly and completely disappeared, and De Castro, for the first time, realised that his confederate had double-crossed him. He knew that the diamonds were at the Safe Deposit, but in what name he hadn't the faintest idea. His only hope of laying his hands on the stones was to find Radiant Keller, and this he could not do. And here ends the first part of the case.

'The second part, of which we're chiefly concerned with the ultimate result, begins nearly two years later, in Cairo. By devious routes and under various names, Amos Keller had eventually reached the City by the Desert. He had plenty of money, the proceeds of past robberies, which he had taken care to bring with him, so financially he had nothing to worry about. At the same time, he was by no means free from care.

'He knew very well that his erstwhile partner, Adolf De Castro, would leave no stone unturned to trace him, and run him to earth at the first available opportunity; and this fact was a constantly present dread which overshadowed the whole of his future existence. He was perfectly well aware of the fate in store for him in the event of De Castro discovering his whereabouts. Many times during his travels, he had attempted to screw up his courage sufficiently to return to London and retrieve the stones, but his fear of De Castro had always retained the upper hand, and he had decided to wait.

'You're probably wondering how it is that I've come into possession of all these facts, but as I continue, I'll make that clear to you. However, to return to the story.

'In the meanwhile Adolf De Castro had never for a single instant during those two years given up his search for Keller, his hatred increasing with the passing time, and at last chance threw in his way a clue to the latter's whereabouts. A mutual friend of both De Castro and Radiant Keller returned from a holiday during which he had visited Egypt, and casually mentioned that he had seen a man who was the living double of Keller in Cairo, but had had no chance of speaking to him. De Castro immediately decided to follow up this faint clue, and the next day set out on his journey East.

'Now we come to the point where James Lessard appears on the scene. He had just concluded some excavation work at Luxor, and was breaking his journey at Cairo on his way home. Returning to Shepheard's Hotel, where he was staying, late one evening, through one of the evil-smelling side-streets with which the town abounds, he had been attracted by the sound of a scuffling noise under a dark archway, and a cry for help in an Englishman's voice. Lessard immediately went to the rescue. A man's figure was lying on the ground, and bending over him were three dusky forms. Evidently the man had been attacked by native thieves.

At Lessard's approach, the men took to their heels. The man on the ground had fainted apparently from loss of blood from a knife wound in the breast. Lessard managed to secure assistance and the man was conveyed to hospital. The next day, a message was sent round to Lessard's hotel to the effect that the man whom he had rescued the previous night was not expected to live, and desired to see him urgently.

'Lessard went round to the hospital at once, and Radiant Keller (for the dying man was he), told him in confidence the whole story, and gave into Lessard's keeping the two little steel balls with full instructions as to their use. Part of these facts I ascertained from an agent of mine in Cairo, in answer to a cable I'd sent; the rest I've deduced from what occurred later. An hour after having made Lessard his confidant, Amos Keller died, and on the morning of the same day, Adolf de Castro arrived in Cairo. Amos Keller had, ever since his disappearance from London, been kept closely under observation by the police, who were perfectly aware of his identity; but as he had been apparently running straight, they had no cause to molest him in any way. But after his death, the papers in some way got hold of his real identity, and published a short paragraph concerning him.

'This was read by Adolf De Castro with what feelings of dismay you can imagine. After having travelled all the way to Cairo, he found himself no nearer to laying his hands upon the Vandevere diamonds than he had been before. Keller must have warned James Lessard concerning De Castro and possibly described him in detail, no doubt laying particular stress upon the fact that De Castro was a dangerous man who would stick at nothing to gain his own ends. I'm convinced that Lessard was unaware that the box contained stolen gems. Had he known this fact, he would undoubtedly have at once communicated with the police. Amos Keller, although making a confidant of Lessard in every other way, I am sure, omitted any mention of the Vandevere diamonds, merely stating that the contents of the box were jewels of considerable value.

'What happened to send him hurrying away that same night, we can only conjecture. Personally, I believe that he caught sight of De Castro somewhere in the street, and recognised him from Keller's description. Whatever it was, he left, and apparently hurried at once to seek the advice of his oldest friend, Harold Brennan. We do know for a fact that he went straight to Liverpool, for the date on which he left Cairo and the date on which, according to Mrs. Lessard's story, he arrived at Brennan's house — the night he was closeted so long with her father in the surgery — correspond, inasmuch as the time between was exactly that which would have been occupied on the journey.

'Now we're bound to enter into a realm of conjecture, although the events which took place after do much to substantiate our suppositions. What exactly happened at the interview between Lessard and his friend, it is impossible to say. But if we consider the words heard by Mrs. Lessard as she passed the surgery door, in conjunction with the fact that we know one of the steel balls was found concealed in James Lessard's tooth, it is at least possible to imagine a good part.

'My own idea is that Lessard, having told Brennan his story, and having impressed upon him the danger in which he stood from De Castro, suggested, so that there should be nothing tangible to connect himself with the dead jewel thief, that Brennan should take possession of the two steel balls, the key to the box containing the jewels, until such time as Lessard was convinced that danger from De Castro no longer existed, and it was safe to redeem the stones from their resting place at the Deposit.

'I'm convinced, Mrs. Lessard, that it was your father who suggested that the balls should be concealed, one in Lessard's left canine tooth, and one in his own. He was a dentist, and it was far more likely to have occurred to him for that reason. However, whoever thought of it, it was a most ingenious hiding place, and in all probability would have served the purpose for which it was intended. De Castro would have been put completely off the scent but for the unfortunate fact that Brennan's assistant, Paul Harte, overheard sufficient of the conversation to make him curious as to its meaning. I don't think he heard enough to let him understand what the steel balls were for, but I do know that he was aware that they were hidden in the teeth, and that they formed some sort of a key to a box in the Safe Deposit. You must bear particularly in mind that Lessard, although he knew that danger threatened him from De Castro, was at the same time unaware exactly how much De Castro knew concerning the steel balls and their use. As a matter of fact, at that time, De Castro was entirely oblivious of their existence. He must, however, have discovered the name of the man who had been last with Amos Keller before his death, and possibly concluded that Keller had not died without making some statement concerning the stolen jewels.

'The sudden departure of Lessard from Cairo probably tended in his mind to confirm this conjecture. At any rate, he followed Lessard to Liverpool and discovered that he was friendly with Brennan. De Castro — who, by the way, at one time was a particularly skilful dentist himself changed his name to that of Doctor Robert Manning, and in his efforts to discover whether Radiant Keller had made a confidant of Lessard — struck up a friendship with Brennan's assistant, Harte. This he assiduously cultivated, and succeeded one evening in learning from Harte of the curious conversation he had overheard between Lessard and the dentist in the surgery.

'It was the vital information that he had been searching for, for such a long time, and his only concern now was to possess himself of the two little balls which gave him access to the stolen diamonds. And then came a shattering blow for Manning, as we'll now call him.

'Harold Brennan suddenly and completely disappeared, and the doctor's plans were set at nought. What happened to Brennan I must confess was a problem that bothered me considerably at first, but I gave a great deal of thought to its solution; and with the help of an agent of mine in Liverpool, with whom I have been in almost daily touch, unknown even to my secretary, I succeeded in elucidating the mystery.

'The disappearance of Brennan is, as a matter of fact, quite simply explained, and but for the fact that it seemed to fit in with the other pieces of the puzzle, has, as a matter of fact, no connection with the problem at all. Brennan had, as we know, complained to his daughter concerning his health; in fact, he had told her he was worried about it. It suddenly occurred to me that in this possibly lay the explanation of his extraordinary disappearance.

'I got immediately in touch with my agent, and after some enquiries, he informed me that on a date corresponding to the one on which the dentist disappeared, a man answering to his description had been admitted to a hospital in Manchester suffering from loss of memory, apparently brought about by a slight blow on his head. The mark still remained. He had, however, been released on the following day, having, it seemed, remembered his identity and given the name of Walters. Why he should have given this name is the only thing I can't account for.'

'It was my mother's maiden name,' interposed Mrs. Lessard quietly.

'Thank you, Mrs. Lessard,' said the professor as he resumed. 'The blow on the head, of course, could have been caused in several ways. He may have slipped and fallen, or have been knocked down by some vehicle and received a jar, which coming on the top of his admitted ill health was enough to upset the delicate mechanism of the brain. In this state, he must have mechanically wandered to the station and taken a ticket for Manchester.

'Manning was now as far off the diamonds as ever. He'd certainly gathered a piece of information that he hadn't possessed before — namely, the existence of the steel balls and their use in gaining access to the Safe Deposit. But he also knew that they were concealed, one in Lessard's tooth and the other in Brennan's, and the latter had vanished, no one knew whither. One ball without the other was useless, and he found himself at a dead end.

'The only piece of satisfaction was the knowledge Manning possessed that Lessard was just as helpless as he was himself. With the luck dead against him, he at last gave up his fruitless efforts to gain possession of the Vandevere diamonds, and three years passed. Then fate — coincidence, or whatever you like to call it — suddenly took a hand in the game, and veered round in Manning's favour.

'One day he came face to face with the missing Brennan! You must remember that during his friendship with Harte, he'd often seen the dentist, and had no difficulty in recognising him. He followed him and discovered that he was living, still in the name of Walters, at some rooms just off Clapham Common. The sight of Brennan must have instantly reawakened in Manning the desire to possess himself of the enormous fortune which now lay within his reach.

'With the assistance of a man named Jim Pearson, whom he picked up at Yellow Batt's Limehouse den, where he was well known, Manning engaged the house on North Side. And then he made his first mistake. During the intervening three years, he'd lost sight of Lessard — you must remember that Manning had never actually seen him — but the doctor had a slight acquaintance with a man, who by the way, knew him as Adolf De Castro, a man who was, as a matter of fact, quite a respectable person and who would have been intensely shocked had he known the real character of his friend. Manning had heard this man mention a James Lessard, who was a member of his club, and concluded that it was the same Lessard, and through his friend, succeeded in getting an introduction. In the meanwhile, Manning and Jim Pearson, who, although he knew nothing about the doctor's real project, had been promised a substantial sum of money for his assistance, succeeded in waylaying Brennan one night on Clapham Common and conveying him to the house on North Side, where Manning extracted the tooth and removed the little steel ball it contained, afterwards keeping the unfortunate dentist a close prisoner.

'The blow on his head which Manning and his accomplice had had to administer in order to overcome Brennan, however, produced a curious result. It completely restored his lost memory, but at the same time left his mind a blank as to the passing of the intervening space of time. He took up the thread of his life from the point where it had been broken — the evening he had taken his fateful walk, on which he had disappeared.

'Manning, having taken possession of the steel ball, now set out to get the other; and the opportunity arrived as he thought, when the note was brought to Lessard at his club from the woman, making the appointment on the Albert Embankment. You will remember, Evens, that Sergeant Wilson discovered that De Castro was present when this note was handed to Lessard.

'There is no doubt that Manning read the note when it was opened by Lessard, and the doctor swiftly laid his plans. No better opportunity was ever likely to present itself at that time in the afternoon. The fog was fairly thick, and Manning concluded that by nightfall, it would grow sufficiently dense to completely cover his movements. He phoned to the woman — whom he had heard Lessard mention more than once — in Lessard's name, cancelling the appointment, and from the time Lessard left the club to the time he met his death on the Albert Embankment at the hands of Manning, the doctor followed him, waiting during the time Lessard spent over dinner at Bolton's flat, in Victoria, watching the place for him to come out.

'But a shock awaited Manning. On extracting the tooth, he found that it was a perfectly sound one, and had never in any way been tampered with! A brief examination of the remainder showed that none had been crowned at all. The man's feelings can be imagined. All his careful scheming had come to nothing, and boiling with fury, he hurried back as fast as possible to his house at Clapham, determined to learn the truth from the old dentist.

'Brennan, although his memory had returned, must have been still in a somewhat hazy state from the result of the blow, and it cannot have taken Manning long to learn the identity and residence of the real Lessard. Having waited so long, he apparently determined that he would lose no more time, and decided to set out for Copthorn House that very morning. The fog, as you know, started clearing about three o'clock so that his journey to Reigate was comparatively easy.

'He used a small two-seater car, which we have lately discovered he hired occasionally from a garage at Clapham Junction, and which he had used all the preceding day. Lessard, as was often his habit according to his man Watts' story, was sitting up reading; and Manning, gaining access as we know by the pantry window, killed him with an old dagger taken from the set in the hall — his own knife, a relic of his student days, he had accidentally left behind on the Embankment — but once more luck was against him. In his flight after extracting the tooth, he fell and lost it among the undergrowth in a small clearing in the trees surrounding the house.

'Dawn was near breaking by this time, and it was dangerous for him to linger any longer, but he determined to remain near at hand and make a search for the tooth later when darkness had again fallen. And of course, it was his face which you, Evens, saw looking in through the study window. In the meanwhile, Brennan had succeeded in escaping from the house on North Side, and with a very natural impulse made direct for his old friend's house at Reigate. He arrived in time to recognise his daughter as she was walking up the road, and ran after her, but she was frightened and fled. He followed, but seeing her in the middle of a group of strange people — ourselves — stayed at the foot of the drive, and later ran into Manning on his return to search for the tooth. Manning recognised him, and realising that all was lost if Brennan was found and questioned, shot him. The rest, I think, you all know.'

Barrington paused at the conclusion of his long story, and selected a fresh cigar. Inspector Evens was the first to break the silence which followed.

'By Jove, Professor!' he grunted. 'You've worked it out cleverly. The whole thing's quite clear now. I'm hanged if I can see how you discovered it all.'

The scientist smiled faintly. 'I must admit, my dear Evens,' he replied, 'that at one time it certainly appeared to be an almost impossible problem, and had I not lighted on a clue at the outset which put me on the right track, we should all probably still be in the dark.'

'What was that, sir?' asked Bobbie interestedly.

'A small detail, Bobbie,' answered Barrington. 'The letter signed A. De Castro, which was found in the pocket of the first Lessard. The name sounded familiar to me, but it was some time before I remembered that it was the same as that of the man who had supplied Amos Keller with an alibi in the Vandevere diamond robbery. That at once connected the two crimes.

'I must admit I was puzzled over the first murder, because the tooth had been left behind, and had obviously been untouched; but directly we came to the second murder, at Copthorn House, and found that the tooth in this case was missing, I started to put two and two together. Why had the tooth been taken? The answer was obviously because it was, or contained, something of value to the criminal. But what? Now a tooth is not a large object, and I at once ruled out the supposition that its contents were of any intrinsic value. The case of the Vandevere robbery was already linked with that of the murders, and it was not an impossible supposition to conclude that the contents of the tooth related in some way to the diamonds.

'My first theory was that the tooth

contained some sort of plan revealing their whereabouts. Then Mrs. Lessard arrived on the scene, and told her strange story. Obviously, whatever secret existed, it was shared between her father and Lessard. With the killing of Brennan and the discovery that his tooth had also been extracted only some days previously, I began to obtain a vague glimmer of the truth. Without any doubt, whatever the secret was, it had evidently been divided between him and Lessard — part in each tooth.

'It was the only solution. I was then fortunate enough to gain possession of the tooth, extracted from Lessard, which Manning in his flight had dropped. And, as you are aware, on removing the gold filling, I discovered the little steel ball. It began to come clear that the first murder was a mistake, owing to the two men possessing the same name. At that time, of course, I had not the remotest idea of the real meaning of the little balls, although I guessed that they were in some way connected with the stolen diamonds.

'I looked up the index, and read up the

account of the robbery, and my memory of the name of Adolf De Castro had not played me false. I also got you, Evens, to let me have a record of Amos Keller, which included an account of his death at Cairo, and incidentally mentioned the name of James Lessard as being with him at the time of his death. I was now fairly convinced that my theory was the right one. As soon as I heard Doctor Manning mention the Safe Deposit at Victoria, in the room at Margrave Street, the whole thing became obvious. I at once went and interviewed the manager, and from him I learned the story of the steel balls.

'I was certain that at the first available opportunity, Manning, now that he was in possession of the key, would make a move to recover the gems. He acted entirely as I had anticipated, but unfortunately at the time he got away. I think that explains everything.

'Except,' said Moira, 'that I can't understand why my husband should have suddenly sent for me.'

'I think I can account for that, too,' answered Barrington, smiling across at her, 'although of course I can't be certain. In a book in his desk, I discovered a scrap of paper bearing the letters S.T.R.O. The last part of the name Adolf De Castro. I'm inclined to believe that in some way he'd been notified that De Castro was in London, and had been making enquiries about James Lessard. The fact had awakened all his dread of the man, and he sent for you to warn you of what might happen, possibly to tell you the whole story.'

'But,' interjected Wallace Manton, 'when he knew, after the disappearance of Moira's — er — Mrs. Lessard's father, that it was impossible for him to gain possession of the jewels, why didn't he inform the police?'

'I think,' said Barrington, 'his reason was that he didn't know why Brennan had so suddenly vanished, and there was always the possibility that he might return again, and so enable them to gain possession of the box.'

'As usual, you've got an answer for everything,' grunted Evens as he raised his neglected glass and drained the contents down his capacious throat.

'I think it's wonderful the way Mr. Barrington's pieced the whole story together,' said Moira, a light of admiration shining in her violet eyes as she gazed at the scientist.

'How was it you were able to find out the first part of the story, sir?' asked Bobbie.

'Partly, as I've said, from Cairo and Liverpool agents who, working for us scientists, gather varied knowledge in doing so,' said Barrington. 'And partly from the lips of Manning himself when I questioned him, and in doing so, practically let me know that I knew the truth. He filled in the gaps, and confessed the whole story.'

For some seconds they all remained silent, gazing into the dying fire. Then the stillness of the room was broken by the sharp, shrill summons of the telephone.

Hertford crossed to the instrument and took down the receiver. 'Hold the line — I'll tell him,' he said a moment later, and turned to Inspector Evens. 'You're wanted — the Yard.'

With an exclamation that sounded

261

suspiciously uncomplimentary to Scotland Yard, Evens heaved his bulky form out of the chair and took the earpiece from Hertford's hand. 'Yes,' he barked, 'this is Inspector Evens.' A short pause, then: 'What!' Another pause. 'Right; I'll go straight to Bow Street now.' Excitedly, the Scotland Yard man banged the receiver on its hook, and turned to Barrington. 'Manning's cheated us after all, Professor,' he said. 'Bow Street phoned the Yard, and they phoned on here. He poisoned himself in his cell — was found dead about half an hour ago. They say the stuff was concealed in the heel of his shoe. I'm going down straight away.' As he spoke, the worthy inspector was struggling into his coat, and the next second, with a hurried goodnight he dashed from the room.

As the door shut behind Barrington rose from his chair and for some minutes stood gazing out of the window with unseeing eyes at the wet and muddy street below. At last, with a shrug of his shoulders, he returned to his chair and sank wearily into it.

'Perhaps, after all, it was for the best,' he murmured, and slowly twisted the ring on his finger.

*   *   *

It was some six months later, and the cold rain and fog of winter had given way to a beautiful spring, hopeful indication of the summer to follow.

In Welbeck Street, with windows flung wide to the morning air, Professor Barrington and his secretary were discussing the prophecy of a certain fellow scientist of vast earthquakes which were supposed to take place shortly.

It was some time since Doctor Manning had succeeded in evading the earthly penalty for his many crimes, and already the case had begun to fade from the minds both the chief characters concerned in it. Hertford was busily engaged in reading the various opinions of famous geologists on the forthcoming holocaust, and Barrington was methodically opening his morning mail as he talked. Suddenly Bobbie looked up in time to see a smile break the grimness of his employer's firm mouth.

'What is it, sir?' he asked.

'An echo, Bobbie,' said the scientist as he tossed the card he had been reading across to his secretary.

It was an invitation to the wedding of Moira Lessard and Wallace Manton.

'It's only what I expected,' Bobbie remarked. 'And if I wasn't so happy with you, sir, I wouldn't mind being the bridegroom myself. I believe I'd make a very good husband.'

To which words of doubtful wisdom the professor made no reply.

THE FACELESS ONES
GRIM DEATH
MURDER IN MANUSCRIPT
THE GLASS ARROW
THE THIRD KEY
THE ROYAL FLUSH MURDERS
THE SQUEALER
MR. WHIPPLE EXPLAINS
THE SEVEN CLUES
THE CHAINED MAN
THE HOUSE OF THE GOAT
THE FOOTBALL POOL MURDERS
THE HAND OF FEAR
SORCERER'S HOUSE
THE HANGMAN
THE CON MAN
MISTER BIG
THE JOCKEY
THE SILVER HORSESHOE
THE TUDOR GARDEN MYSTERY
THE SHOW MUST GO ON
SINISTER HOUSE
THE WITCHES' MOON
ALIAS THE GHOST
THE LADY OF DOOM

THE BLACK HUNCHBACK
PHANTOM HOLLOW
WHITE WIG
THE GHOST SQUAD
THE NEXT TO DIE
THE WHISPERING WOMAN
THE TWELVE APOSTLES
THE GRIM JOKER
THE HUNTSMAN
THE NIGHTMARE MURDERS
THE TIPSTER
THE VAMPIRE MAN
THE RED TAPE MURDERS
THE FRIGHTENED MAN
THE TOKEN
MR. MIDNIGHT
THE RIVER MEN

With Chris Verner:
THE BIG FELLOW
THE SNARK WAS A BOOJUM
THE SEVENTH VIRGIN

We do hope that you have enjoyed reading this large print book.

Did you know that all of our titles are available for purchase?

We publish a wide range of high quality large print books including:
Romances, Mysteries, Classics
General Fiction
Non Fiction and Westerns

Special interest titles available in large print are:
The Little Oxford Dictionary
Music Book, Song Book
Hymn Book, Service Book

Also available from us courtesy of Oxford University Press:
Young Readers' Dictionary
(large print edition)
Young Readers' Thesaurus
(large print edition)

For further information or a free brochure, please contact us at:
Ulverscroft Large Print Books Ltd.,
The Green, Bradgate Road, Anstey,
Leicester, LE7 7FU, England.
Tel: (00 44) **0116 236 4325**
Fax: (00 44) **0116 234 0205**

Other titles in the
Linford Mystery Library:

VILLAGE OF FEAR

Noel Lee

After narrowly escaping death on a train, two people find themselves in an eerie deserted village — and make a grisly discovery . . . On a dark and stormy night, locals gather in an inn to tell a frightening tale . . . A writer's country holiday gets off to a bad start when he finds a corpse in his cottage . . . And a death under the dryer at a fashionable hairdressing salon leads to several beneficiaries of the late lady's will falling under suspicion of murder . . .

PUNITIVE ACTION

John Robb

Soldiers of Fort Valeau, a Foreign Legion outpost, discover the mutilated bodies of several men from their overdue relief column, ambushed and massacred by Dylaks. Captain Monclaire's radio report to the garrison at Dini Sadazi results in a promise that more soldiers will be despatched to Valeau, from there to mount punitive action against the offenders. But before the reinforcements arrive, the Dylaks send a message to Monclaire — if he does not surrender, they will attack and conquer the fort . . .

DEATH WALKS SKID ROW

Michael Mallory

Sunset Boulevard, 1975: Two men are speeding home from a party on a night that will haunt them forever. Despite the dangerously wet roads, both passenger and driver are very drunk. Thirty years later on Los Angeles's Skid Row, a homeless man is found dead in an alley. Discovering several disturbing connections, reporter Ramona Rios and a man known on Skid Row only as 'the governor' set out on separate paths to unveil the truth, but are brought together to face a perilous web of power, manipulation and deceit.

ONCE YOU STOP, YOU'RE DEAD

Eaton K. Goldthwaite

The USS *Slocum* is on a routine naval patrol northwest of Bermuda when the SOS crackles over the radio. Cuban National Air's Flight Twelve is ditching in the Atlantic with eighty-nine passengers and five crew aboard. Commander H.P. Perry readies his ship for standard rescue operations — only to discover there's nothing standard about the survivors. Once aboard, they're more demanding than grateful, for most are Russian or Cuban nationals. That's when Commander Perry realizes he's an unwitting pawn in a deadly game, the outcome of which could have grave international repercussions . . .

MURDER GETS AROUND

Robert Sidney Bowen

Murder and mayhem begin innocently enough at the Rankins' cocktail party, where Gerry Barnes and his fiery red-haired girlfriend Paula Grant while away a few carefree hours. There, Gerry meets René DeFoe, who wishes to engage his services as a private investigator, for undisclosed reasons — an assignment Gerry reluctantly accepts. But the next morning, when Gerry enters his office to keep his appointment, he finds René murdered on the premises. He puts his own life at risk as he investigates why a corpse was made of his client . . .

THE FREE TRADERS

Victor Rousseau

The Free Traders deal fur and whisky, debouching their way through the Canadian northern territories. Pitted against them are the country's soldier-police, the Northwest Mounted. Lee Anderson, Royal Canadian Mounted Police sergeant, is on a mission to find a man wanted for murder twenty-five years ago. But when he and a mysterious woman are thrown down a cliff by a dynamite explosion, her memory disappears from the shock, and they find themselves in a wilderness pursued by the Free Traders — who are bent on killing Lee and capturing the woman.